THE LAST OF THE HONEYWELLS

Also by Robert B. Gillespie

The Hell's Kitchen Connection
Empress of Coney Island
Heads You Lose
Print-Out

THE LAST OF THE HONEYWELLS

A Novel of Suspense

Robert B. Gillespie

DODD, MEAD & COMPANY
New York

Copyright © 1988 by Robert B. Gillespie
All rights reserved
No part of this book may be reproduced in any form
without permission in writing from the publisher.
Published by Dodd, Mead & Company, Inc.,
71 Fifth Avenue, New York, N.Y. 10003
Manufactured in the United States of America
First Edition

1 2 3 4 5 6 7 8 9 10

Library of Congress Cataloging-in-Publication Data
Gillespie, Robert B.
   The last of the Honeywells: a novel of suspense / Robert B.
Gillespie.
     p.—cm.
    I. Title.
PS3557.I3795L3 1988
813'.54—dc 19   87-24062
0-396-09266-2   CIP

THE LAST OF THE HONEYWELLS

One

AT SEVEN-THIRTY that morning, Lisa Honeywell swung her red Firebird to a stop in front of her grandfather's place, a frame house on a residential street south of Northern Boulevard in Little Neck. The only thing that distinguished this house from the other houses was the modest plaque on the front door that said: "ANIMAL HOSPITAL, Homer Honeywell, D.V.S."

It was a wonderful June morning, and she was happy. She got out of the car, patted its roof jauntily, sauntered like a boy to the house, and danced up the wooden steps, whistling soundlessly. She was dressed in her usual garb, sneakers, blue jeans, and a short velour jacket. She had three or four such jackets; this was the pink one. She carried a McDonald's take-out bag with an Egg McMuffin in it for her grandfather. Over the last two years she had got in the habit of stopping off several times a week on her way to work with a breakfast of sorts for him because she didn't trust the old man to take care of himself. He was seventy-five and still practicing.

Lisa was an unusual person. At twenty, she shrugged off the fact that she had the most beautiful face within many miles of her home in nearby Savage Point. It was a broad face with large, dark-lashed brown eyes set far apart, a wide mouth, ruddy cheeks which were more a sign of allergies than of coursing good health, and short brown hair which received the barest minimum of combing. When she smiled, which was often, she seemed to light up the neighborhood. It was good to see her smile.

Her grandfather boasted that she had to "beat off the boys with a stick." This was true, sometimes literally, for she wasn't—not yet anyway—interested in wielding the power that her beauty gave her. She was interested in more engrossing things like tinkering with her car's engine and dreaming of racing it in competition out on the Island, fixing things around the house, watching cartoons on television on Saturday mornings, catching shoplifters on her job as store detective. She was also interested in throwing herself into the seasonal sports: skiing, skating, and sledding in the winter; swimming, diving, water-skiing, and sailing in Little Neck Bay in the summer. There was no time for messing with boys. As she told her friend Meg, all they wanted to do was you-know-what.

One of Lisa's drawbacks was a mild dyslexia. Reading was a heavy chore, and since her basic intelligence was no higher than average, this was a serious drawback in middle-class, education-oriented Savage Point. It had taken all of her grit—and the generosity of teachers— to get her through high school. Graduation was a tremendously blessed relief. While most of her classmates at Cardozo High School went on to college, Lisa strolled into a sequence of junky jobs, all of which she performed with gusto. She had been through her period of teenage revolt and had emerged with an acceptance of herself as she was, without approval or disapproval. Her grandfather called her "happy-go-lucky," and she liked the expression. She was Grandpa's girl.

The door to the old veterinarian's office was unlocked. She shook her head and grimaced disapprovingly at this evidence of her grandfather's forgetfulness. Lisa's father wanted the old man to retire. When the subject was brought up, the old man would say in outraged tones, "What would I do—play golf?" as if golf was a disease of the brain, a way of killing not only time but oneself as well.

Lisa's father would say, "But you're entitled to have some fun, Dad, to lie in the sun—"

"Horsefeathers!"

The seventy-five-year-old man had lived alone for years after Grandma died, finding all the companionship he wanted at O'Grady's, the neighborhood bar. Then when his boyhood friend, a retired insurance salesman named Tom Shakespeare, began to show signs of deteriorating health, Homer Honeywell took him into the house to keep an eye on him. When Lisa was small, she couldn't pronounce the name of Grandpa's friend; to her he was Uncle Shaky long before the tremors became noticeable. And the ailing man claimed he was honored to be Lisa's Uncle Shaky.

The unlocked door brought Lisa's mind back to the break-in that had happened a year ago. It had to happen sooner or later, but there was no sense inviting the cokeheads in by leaving the door unlocked, for Pete's sake.

The morning of the break-in a police car had been out front, and two uniformed cops were coming down the steps putting their hats back on as if they were coming from church or a wake. That time Lisa had been bringing not an Egg McMuffin but some sugary stuff from Dunkin' Donuts.

The cops had assured her that her grandfather was all right, but she had rushed in to see for herself, through the bare waiting room into the old-fashioned, not particularly sanitary work center dominated by the white steel all-purpose examining/operating table under one of those new-fangled fluorescent light fixtures, circa 1939. Old wooden cabinets and counters lined the walls except for a large Sears, Roebuck refrigerator with added hoops for a padlock. The only other piece of furniture in the room was a tall barstool which the old man used as a butt rest when he was working.

That time she found her grandfather half-sitting on the stool, a picture of dejection. She had always thought him a handsome man with the classic nose of a matinee idol, but at that moment his rimless glasses had slipped to the tip of his nose, his stubbled face was pale, and the skimpy gray strands of his hair went every which way. He had on a rumpled pair of pants over his pajamas, slippers on his feet. She was shocked to see that he looked like an old man.

She went to him and hugged him, dropping the Dunkin' Donuts bag on the table.

"Are you okay, Gramps?" she asked.

"Fit as a fiddle, fine as silk," he said with false heartiness. "Some shitepoke broke in, that's all." "Shitepoke" was as strong an expletive as he ever used. "Be cleaned up in no time," he said.

4

She looked around, saw cabinets broken open, the refrigerator door gaping, its padlock hanging from a hoop.

"They were after drugs, right?" She didn't have to read to know all about drugs and drug users.

The old man put on his pixy smile. "They weren't after my million-dollar art collection," he said.

"Are the animals all right?" she asked, going to the door leading to the kennels.

He was glaring at the bag on the table. "Come here, Lisa honey," he said. "That isn't more of those damned doughnuts, is it? If it is—"

"A new kind, Gramps, you'll love them," she said. Then she said, "They must have made enough noise to wake the dead. Didn't you hear anything?"

He looked at her blankly. "Aren't you late for work?"

She shrugged. She and her father had been after him to get a hearing aid, and any suggestion of it made the partially deaf old man furious.

She looked around, a frown on her lovely face.

"They took syringes, too, didn't they?" she said.

Her grandfather nodded wearily.

Then she announced, "I know who did it."

"Oh?"

"Brucie," she said with distaste. "Bruce Webster."

He grinned, and she realized why he looked so old. His lower teeth were obviously still in the bathroom upstairs. "So the store detective is smarter than the police," he said, teasing her. "The case is solved by the great store detective."

"I'm serious, Gramps. Anyone can see it was kids looking for uppers. It's happening all over."

The old man sighed heavily. "Uppers? Stimulants? Hallucinogens? All I had were downers, honey. Enough

5

to kill a herd of elephants. Is this Brucie of yours suicidal? Is he tired of living so soon?"

"He's into drugs, Gramps. He gets crazy. I've seen him. He's totally disgusting."

"I thought he was a friend of yours."

"Brucie? Yuk, you gotta be kidding! Not Brucie, Gramps, his sister Meg. Meg's my friend, not that piece of throw-up . . .! Oh, here! Eat your breakfast. I have to go. Get Uncle Shaky to help you clean up. You really ought to retire, you know."

"You're getting as bossy as your father," he said, and turned his head away.

Still fretting about the unlocked door, Lisa paused in the empty waiting room. It looked grubby, terminally abandoned. The wooden benches were scarred, the linoleum floor stained. It smelled. She glanced at the oil painting on the wall and had to smile. It was a pitifully amateurish painting of a room full of animals, mostly cats, though it was hard to tell for sure, reclining peacefully on a daybed and the floor; over them hovered a disembodied human head, presumably a likeness of Dr. Honeywell, with a holy aura emanating from it. Titled "Angel of Mercy," it was the work of an eccentric old woman, known as the Cat Woman of Savage Point, who lavished her love and what money she had on stray animals and brought them to Dr. Honeywell for medication and repair. The embarrassed veterinarian had let his wife hang the painting in the waiting room—she was alive then—and he had never looked at it again.

The painting was pooh-y, Lisa thought, but the title was appropriate. Her grandfather had spent fifty years of his life taking care of animals with an almost saintlike devotion. He still made house calls whenever he could, and it was this peculiarity that made *People* magazine do a story on him several years ago, headed, naturally, "Angel of Mercy." Lisa loved the painting because it made her feel warm inside.

She moved into the operating room, calling, "Gramps?" He wasn't there. Probably still upstairs. She made a tsking sound as she noticed that his diploma from Cornell had fallen to the floor, its frame and glass broken. *Really!* She picked up the parchment and the larger pieces of glass and frame, and put them on a counter.

She went into the front hall and called up the stairs, "Gramps?"

No answer. Still asleep. She made a face in disappointment. She always looked forward to a little lighthearted banter with her grandfather. Back in the operating room, she deposited the Egg McMuffin on the table. Too bad it would be cold when he eventually got to it. With a ballpoint she wrote on the bag in her childish script: "Heat before you eat, dum-dum."

Then following her custom, she went back to the kennels to say hello to the animals before she left. There were three cats and a dog in the metal cages. One cat was too sick to respond to her, another had a bandage around its middle, the third was a beat-up tom. The dog was a filthy little white poodle who yipped.

"Where's Killer?" she asked the poodle. The poodle said yip yip.

She peered in all the cages. The dog she was looking for wasn't really named "Killer," she just called him that affectionately because he was so big and scary looking. Actually he was the gentlest of creatures whose real name was Shep. He belonged to her father's law partner, a big and scary looking but gentle man named

Eddie Epstein. She knew that Uncle Eddie was out of town and wasn't due back until the following week. In the meantime Shep was a star boarder at Dr. Honeywell's Animal Hospital.

But where was he? Could her grandfather have left him in one of the animal runs all night, she wondered. The deep backyard abutted the rear of the stores on Northern Boulevard. Technically "Old Doc" Honeywell's establishment violated the city's zoning laws, but he was so well loved by the neighbors on the block and by the storekeepers that they put up with his presence despite the occasional noise and odors.

Frowning, she opened the door to the backyard. It was really too chilly to leave an animal out all night, she thought. Really, Gramps! There were four long runs enclosed in heavy chicken wire.

At first they appeared to be empty. Then she heard the whimpering and saw Shep cowering at the far end of the nearest run. He was looking at her, pleading, half-barking, the tail whisking tentatively then stopping. His ears were drawn back on his head, and Lisa knew he was frightened.

"Come here, Killer. Come here, baby," she said. The dog took a step toward her, then cowered back.

"What's the matter, boy?" She unlatched the gate to the run.

It was only then that she saw her grandfather lying on the ground. He was dressed in old flannel pajamas. His feet were bare.

She cried, "Gramps!"

Crouching over him, she rolled him onto his back.

Another young woman would have screamed—loud enough to wake the dead, as Lisa might have put it. It took long moments for the horrible sight to register in her brain. Her grandfather's throat was ripped open as if by a lion or a tiger, and the great expanse of bloody tissue under the bloodless face and staring eyes was an obscenity crying to heaven for vengeance.

She must have blacked out for a moment, for she became aware of pushing herself up from the ground. Then she started cursing—great molten hunks of words formed in the fires of hell.

Sometime later she was intoning to anyone who was near, "He didn't do it! Killer didn't do it, goddamnit! Leave him alone! I know he didn't do it!"

Then she heard the shot from the policeman's gun, and that moment marked the beginning of her descent into savagery.

Two

UNCLE SHAKY was no help at all. Lisa had charged up the stairs and roused him out of bed, saying, "Some fucking shitepoke has killed Gramps!" But Tom Shakespeare was aggravatingly slow. She left him while he was still climbing out of bed, thumped back down the stairs, went to the telephone, and dialed 911.

Then she headed back to the animal runs by way of the kennel area. The white poodle yipped excitedly, and Lisa said, "Shut your face!" It was urgent that her grandfather be moved from the run, he didn't belong there in the dirt. But she couldn't bring herself to touch him.

She went past the body to the far end to soothe the German shepherd. "It's all right, Killer. Don't blame you for being spooked." She hugged and petted him. Then she said, "Tell me what happened. Who did it, Shep?" She looked closely at the dog's mouth and paws. No sign of a reversion to a bestial state. Clean.

"People are liable to think the wrong thing, Killer," she said. "Let's get you out of here."

She tried to lead him past the body, but the dog refused. She kept her face averted from the mangled ruins of her beloved grandfather, but the wide-set eyes that gave her the peripheral vision to catch shoplifters betrayed her. The torn throat certainly looked like the work of an animal; there were even what looked like fang marks at the edges of the devastated throat area. Frenziedly she tugged at the dog—and couldn't budge him.

Uncle Shaky appeared at the back door. Lisa called to him to drag her grandfather's body into the house. But the befuddled man just stood there, saying, "I can't believe what I'm seeing. Oh my God, I can't believe it."

Then the police arrived, and Shep's fate was sealed.

Tom Shakespeare ate the Egg McMuffin. He tried to act as if he were in command of the situation, but everything he did was at Lisa's growled command. Because of her sobbing and raging, she couldn't control her voice; Shakespeare's voice, quavering though it was, was clearer. Thus she goaded the old man into making the necessary phone calls.

Tom Shakespeare was a large wreck of a man, obese almost to the point of grossness, unable because of his ailments to do much exercising, and unwilling to put limits on his appetite. "It's my only pleasure, my dear niece-a Lisa," he once said to her. "So what if I die young." Breezily. He was seventy-five, the same age as her grandfather.

Between bouts of screeching at the police, she had Shakespeare put in a call to her father's office in Albany.

Marcus Honeywell was the state assemblyman from the district and spent much of his time in the state capital. She also had Shakespeare call Bill Greaney, the funeral director. Her grandfather had delighted in poking fun at Greaney for his fatuous insincerity, but he had liked the man all the same.

Then she had Uncle Shaky call the owners of the animals in the kennels. The three cats belonged to the Cat Woman, who was now so old that she imposed on a long-suffering neighbor to run her errands for her. It was the neighbor who eventually came to retrieve the cats. The white poodle belonged to Jack Doran, the charming newcomer to Savage Point who in little more than two years had built a thriving business tending to the lawns in the area. Shakespeare left a message on his answering machine.

Nothing could be done about Shep, whom the police had just "put to sleep" by slamming a bullet into his brain. The owner, Eddie Epstein, was divorced and lived alone. Since he was out of town, there was no rush, the dog was dead.

Lisa glared at the large policeman who bore the stolid face of dumb rectitude. "Why did you have to shoot him?" she demanded. "He didn't do it."

"He was a killer, missy," the policeman explained in a kindly tone. "An outlaw, a renegade. Once they get a taste of blood—"

"But there was no blood on him!"

The policeman gave her a tight smile. "Dogs are good at cleaning themselves. Now don't you worry your head about him."

She lost control and called him a thick-headed shitepoke.

The policeman wouldn't talk to her after that, so she forced Tom Shakespeare to raise the question of an autopsy. The sergeant in charge grimaced and said that the cause of death was obvious. When a reporter from *Newsday* arrived on the scene, the sergeant realized that the victim was someone more important than just an old nobody who had gotten careless with a killer dog, and he agreed to recommend an autopsy.

Lisa's rage abated. She moved about restlessly, with Tom Shakespeare plodding after her. She picked up her grandfather's rumpled diploma, discolored with age. She couldn't tell if the script was in English or Latin. She rolled it up and handed it to Shakespeare. "I want this, Uncle Shaky," she said. "Keep it for me."

She glanced up at the wall space between the cabinets where the diploma had been hanging. The hook was still solidly in place. She wondered dully how the diploma could have fallen when the hook was still there.

Shakespeare said something.

Lisa said, "What?"

He gave her a sad smile. "I was just saying that the sheepskin gets old just as we do."

"Oh, you mean the diploma."

He nodded.

The Cat Woman's neighbor came with three cat carriers for the cats. "The old girl is broken up," he said, wagging his head mournfully. "She worshiped the doc."

The little white yipper was picked up by Jack Doran's son Paul. Paul, the same age as Lisa, was one of the young men she had beaten off with a stick, a sharp one to the stomach when they were both seniors at Cardozo. She didn't know whether she liked him or not. As she had said to Meg, "All he ever thinks about is making out." Meg hadn't said anything, and Lisa wondered if nice but homely Meg welcomed Paul's attention. It was just that Paul was so stuck-up about his tanned, handsome face, his white-toothed smile and trim, muscular body. This male arrogance posing as charm put Lisa off.

And yet she felt a kinship of sorts with him. Like her, he was a poor student who hadn't gone on to college. Instead, he had worked for a while with his father in the yard beautification business, then perhaps figuring he had had enough of his old man, had left to become a security guard patroling Savage Point. The similarity of their jobs was another point in common between them.

He showed up at the animal hospital in his guard uniform. Holding the obnoxious little dog in one arm, he took Lisa to the front porch away from the haunting emptiness inside.

"Sorry about your grandfather," he said.

"Yeah, me too."

"If there's anything I can do—"

"Thanks just the same, Paulie," she said. "I've been wondering. Why don't you give that dumb dog a bath?"

Paul made a face. "He don't like it. He bites."

"I wouldn't keep a dog who bites," she said.

He looked down at the dog. "He's Poppa's dog, not mine . . . You're a mean little bastard, aren't you, you little fucker?" The two glared at each other.

Lisa said, "If I were you, I'd accidentally run over him."

She went back inside. There wasn't anything for her to do. The police had taken away both bodies, her grandfather's and the dog's, but several of the cops were still hanging around. They didn't seem to know what to do, either.

Tom Shakespeare was on the phone. He handed it to her.

"Talk to your father," he said.

She said, "Hi, Pops," and started to cry silently.

Her father said soothing things to her.

"They killed Shep," she said.

He said something about police procedure.

She said that Shep didn't do it.

He said that reminded him to call Eddie Epstein, but that he would do it when Epstein got back to the city. No rush, the dog was dead. He said he was leaving Albany as soon as he could get away in the afternoon, he would fly his Lear to Flushing Airport, pick up his car, and probably be home by six. She said okay.

She loved and idolized her dashing father, but she had never gotten on intimate terms with him. He was fun to be with, particularly in the last couple of years—They went cruising on the boat together when he wasn't using it for political purposes, they did many things together—but they never really confided in each other about the things that counted most, their feelings. When her mother had moved out of the house to open a successful bathroom boutique on Manhattan's Madison Avenue, all her father had said to Lisa was, "It was something your mother had to do, honey, it doesn't mean she doesn't love you." *Ha,* Lisa had thought.

What was she supposed to do now? Hang around her grandfather's office with old Shakespeare who used to tell interesting stories but was now in a state of shock? He kept saying he couldn't believe it. Six hours of hearing him say he couldn't believe it? Eek! Go upstairs and mess around with her grandfather's things? She couldn't bring herself to do that, not yet. Go home to the empty house and do what? Grieve? Clean her room? Listen to the yammering cleaning women? Lie down and cry her head off? The hell with that.

She decided to go to work, if only for a few hours.

She drove her Firebird to the mammoth Roosevelt Field Shopping Center and found a parking space about a half mile from Macy's, where she worked.

She roamed through the huge department store in a dreamlike state. The whole day was unreal. She would go home and her grandfather would still be there.

She watched a black woman go into the dressing room with two dresses and come out with only one. Her mind worked slowly. What am I supposed to do now? What would Killer do? Wag his tail, that's what, and wait to be petted. He'd never go for anyone's throat, because he was just a big old pussycat.

She put her hand on the woman's arm, and the woman slugged her on the head with her pocketbook. Lisa wasn't sure what happened next, but her boss pulled her off the woman and sent her home. "We apprehend them," he said. "We don't try to break their arm."

Midafternoon she became aware that she was parked in front of Ralph Simmons's house on Dover Street in Savage Point. This was crazy—the only person in the whole world she could talk to, really talk to, was an old man she wasn't even related to! Well, not really so old, not half as old as Gramps, maybe in his early sixties, and his hair was hardly gray at all. She had known him all her life, it seemed, and somehow he was always there to talk to when she had things on her mind. She didn't know why, just that he never preached at her the way some other people she could mention did, and he listened good. He never came across like, I've lived three times as long as you and so I'm three times smarter. Maybe it was the way he acted—like he was still young, you know?

She sat in the car with her head bowed. She really shouldn't bother Uncle Ralph with her troubles. Down at the end of Dover Street the sun glinted off the water of Little Neck Bay. Savage Point was a neck of land sticking out into the bay, part of New York City yet constantly on a war alert against the insensitive city bureaucrats who wanted to change it to an area of highrise condos. What it was, it was a nice smug middleclass community, and the residents wanted to keep it that way.

Ralph Simmons in sweater and slacks came out of the house, an old frame house in need of paint, and walked down the path to Lisa's car. Pudgy was the word for his figure, not fat, just overweight from the indulgent application of dry martinis over too many years. His face, ordinarily round and sunny, was somewhat overcast.

"We heard," he said. "Come on in, sweetie."

"You sure?" she asked.

He opened the door for her. "I bet you haven't had any lunch," he said.

She climbed out of the car, and gave him a fierce hug. "I don't want to bother Aunt Lillian," she said.

With an arm around her shoulder, he led her up the path. "No bother. Fixing food is her way of playing. Like a kid with mud pies."

"Mud pies?"

"Didn't you ever make mud pies?"

"Not that I remember."

"You poor underprivileged kid," he said.

She laughed for the first time on that terrible day. And out of the blue she remembered the time she had snarled at him. It was during the turbulence of her fifteenth year, maybe her sixteenth. Ralph Simmons was living alone in the big house. It was after his first wife had died and before he married his former secretary, Lillian Caplin. Lisa knew he was drinking too much at the time, but it was only later that she realized he was going through a crisis almost as awful as her own.

Even now at twenty, she had no insight into herself and the powerful emotions that were raging through her at fifteen. All she knew was that her parents were the enemy and she had to escape their tyranny or she would be forced to kill herself. Her mother, who was still living at home at the time, was the more demanding one. The woman was fixated on Lisa's messy room and choice of clothing; she wanted Lisa to wear proper skirts and blouses and on dressier occasions the lovely gowns that she insisted on buying for her. It made no difference, they all wound up on the floor of Lisa's room.

Lisa explained that one doesn't wear skirts on motorcycles, and her mother went into a screeching fit. Lisa was running around with one of the wilder groups of boys at the time, kids who were into pot, wine, and loud bikes.

That particular battle reached a climax when one of the boys splattered himself on the rocks beneath the Shore Road sea wall in the delusion that his bike was a flying machine. The Honeywell house was on Shore Road a short distance from where the flying motorcycle crashed, and Lisa's parents heard of the death only minutes after it happened. Her mother misunderstood and, believing that Lisa had been on the bike with the boy, became hysterical. Shortly after that her mother left home, and Lisa started to edge her way out of the wild bunch. The hot war of her teenage revolt abated.

What sent her mother packing was the night of the joyride. Lisa was in a stew about something and decided to work it off by taking a spin in the family car, a sleek and speedy Thunderbird. Her friend Meg Webster refused to ride with her, and Lisa called her chicken, but Meg's brother Bruce said he'd be happy to take a joyride with Lisa. So Lisa showed off for Brucie until he started to climb all over her at a lookout point somewhere on the South Shore, and she had to grab and squeeze his marbles to make him stop.

Then she was alone in the car, and it was late at night—around midnight—and she was running out of gas. She figured she had punished her parents enough and headed for home. As she came down Shore Road from the north she saw with a shock just how much her parents loved her—there was a police car parked in front of the house!

She gunned the T-bird past the house and kept going to the only haven that she knew of, Ralph Simmons's house on Dover Street. Ralph had a drink in his hand when he came to the door, and behind him the color TV was tuned to "The Johnny Carson Show."

"I have only one question to ask, Uncle Ralph," she said. "Can I stay in one of your spare rooms tonight? Answer yes or no."

Ralph peered at her for a moment in silence, then said, "Well, don't just stand there. Come on in."

She entered, glowering. "The cops are after me," she said.

"So you need a hide-out . . . Are you hungry?"

"Sort of."

He turned off the television and sat her down in the living room. He went to the kitchen and heated some leftover pasta in the microwave oven. When he returned, she was scowling at him.

"Can I?" she demanded to know.

He put the food down and sat opposite her. "Don't you think you should call your parents?" he asked.

"No, they don't care about me. They just want to keep me in jail."

"Jail?"

"The house. My father wouldn't let me out the front door. So I went out the back. Ha, ha to him."

"So this is a jailbreak?"

"Yeah, sort of."

"And you think because the police are there they want to put you in a real jail?"

"They'll say I stole the car. It's my car as much as it is theirs."

"But you don't have a license."

"I can drive." Sullenly, defiantly.

"The only reason they called the police is because they're worried about you. The least you can do is call them and tell them you're all right."

"Without telling them where I am?"

"If that's what you want."

"Does that mean I can stay here?"

"Only if you call them."

She said, "They don't care about me."

"Your dog will miss you."

"Not till morning. Poochie's asleep."

"Tell me, when you take Poochie out for a walk, why do you keep him on a leash?"

"That's silly. So he won't get run over by a car. And so he won't do his poops on somebody's lawn."

"But wouldn't Poochie rather be free and go wherever he wants to go without you holding him back?"

"I suppose so. I never asked him."

"Do you love Poochie?"

"Of course I do. What a silly question."

"So you hold him back because you love him and don't want him to get hurt."

"Are you comparing me to a dog?"

(Sighing) "In a way. I'm just trying to show you that your parents hold you back not because they want to be mean but because they love you and don't want you to get hurt."

(Sullenly) "I can take care of myself."

"I'm sure you can, but you're causing your parents a lot of pain."

(Angrily) "So I'll call them! You're as bad as they are! So I'll call them! But I won't tell them where I am, okay? Okay?"

So she stayed the night at Ralph Simmons's house. That was a long time ago, and times change. Poochie died peacefully, and Lisa matured.

When Aunt Lillian hugged her at the door, it was like being hugged by a large beach ball. She was a small round person with graying blond hair, a glistening, beaming face, and a generous nose. Ordinarily she was bubbling with high spirits, but now she exuded pained sympathy. "You poor dear," she said.

Lisa said, "Cut it out, Aunt Lillian."

Ralph led her to the back porch with the rusted screening, while Lillian fixed her a tuna sandwich and a tall glass of Pepsi.

Lisa said, "My grandfather was murdered."

He said, "How do you figure that, sweetie?"

"Shep didn't do it. Someone tried to make it look like the dog did it, but he didn't."

"But the police—"

She said, "The police are asses, all of them! Answer me this, how can a diploma fall from the wall when the hook is still in there solid and the picture wire isn't broken? How can that happen?"

"You think someone took it down and smashed it?"

"How else?"

When Lisa left at five-thirty, Ralph said, "You need any help, I'm always here. Remember that."

She said, "Thank you, Uncle Ralph." A smile momentarily lit up her face, and Ralph Simmons felt idiotically happy.

Three

MARCUS HONEYWELL was a man of excessive nervous energy. Even while standing still, he was in motion as if acting out his fast-moving thoughts. This genuine openness, this ebullience along with his movie-star good looks and quick wit made him almost romantically attractive to the voters of the area, who had elected him to the Assembly five years ago and reelected him twice since then. He had run as an independent against two stolid characters who were actually more representative of the conservative values of the residents; yet he had won because enough of the voters deemed it a privilege to be represented by so glamorous and likable a person. His opponents charged that he had bought the elections with his wealth but couldn't point to a single vote that had been paid for. The fact that he was one of the few millionaires in the area made him more glamorous, rather than less, to the voters.

Lisa once asked him why he had bothered to become an assemblyman.

His face had broken into a broad grin. "So I'd have an excuse to buy my own plane," he had said. "Commuting to Albany by commercial plane is the pits."

"Why'd you need an excuse? Why not just buy one?"

"That would be what they call conspicuous consumption," he had explained. "I'm a local lawyer, my business is in New York City, in Queens and Manhattan for the most part. I couldn't fly from here to Foley Square even if I wanted to. Do you see what I mean, honey?"

Since she didn't know what "conspicuous consumption" meant, she had simply replied, "Whatever you say, Pops."

The evening of the day she discovered her grandfather's mangled body the police had not yet released the body to the undertaker, so father and daughter were alone together in the big house on Shore Road with no wake to keep them busy, bothered only by the ringing of the telephone. After a while Marcus left it off the hook. "Every damn animal lover in the country wants to get into the act," he grumbled.

They were sitting in sullen exhaustion in the sun room gazing absently at the pleasure boats moored in Little Neck Bay. He jumped to his feet. "Do you know what I need? I need a drink."

She leaped up with him. "Me too."

He looked at her in surprise because she had never liked alcohol. Then he said, "You're entitled."

He made himself a large bone-dry Tanqueray martini. She put together a tall concoction of five sweet cordials, rum and club soda on ice.

Her father made retching sounds. "All that needs is a scoop of ice cream," he said.

"Good idea," she said, and she added some vanilla ice cream from the freezer.

They forced themselves to resume their seats in the sun room, where they sat in uneasy silence.

She said, "What makes marks like a dog's teeth but isn't?"

He said, "I give up. What?"

"Something," she said.

After a while, he said, "I should make some phone calls."

She said, "Wait."

Then she said, "I've been thinking. Grandpa didn't have much money, did he?"

"Enough to get by," her father said. "You knew your grandfather, honey, probably better than I did. Did he ever talk to you about money?"

She thought a moment, then said, "No."

Marcus sighed. "He was a strange man, your grandfather. Probably a saint. That's what the Cat Woman called him."

"Angel."

"Right. Angel."

He went back into the house and made a phone call. When he rejoined her, he said, "Greaney's got him now. We have a couple of rough days ahead of us. Should we go pick out a coffin?"

"No. Gramps wouldn't care what they put him in."

"I care," he said. "You haven't touched your drink, not that I blame you."

She peered at it. "It's pretty, isn't it?"

He said, "I suppose we ought to get something to eat. Where would you like to go?"

Still looking at the drink, now marbled with melting ice cream, she said, "Funny thing about money. You have all of it, and he had none."

Abruptly, he yanked his garden chair near hers and took her hand. "Lisa," he said. "Lisa, honey, that's the way he wanted it, you know that. Why are you brooding about money now, for Pete's sake?"

"To keep from thinking about his murder."

"Okay, let's talk about money. I'd rather do that than go into your murder theory all over again. Okay, money. It all happened before I was born, so all I know is what I was told. Not by Dad. He'd just wave me off and say, Don't worry about it. But by old Paisley the banker. Marcus Paisley, you wouldn't remember him, he died about the time you were born. I think I was named after him."

"It's a nutty name."

"Do you want to talk about money or my nutty name?"

She looked at him sulkily. "I know what you're going to say. He set up a trust for you the day you were born. I know all that. I want to know why."

"You don't know all that, Lisa," he said. "That trust had been set up *before* I was born, and all he did was switch it over to me."

"Why?"

"I don't *know* why! He just did."

"Where'd the money come from?"

"He had it, that's all I know."

"From someone in the family? How much was it?"

"Very little to start with, maybe ten or twenty thousand, I don't know. But old Paisley was a genius. What he did with that money was pure magic. To give you an example, back in the fifties he put a bundle of

26

it in an unknown corporation called Xerox when it was selling for about five. What is it now?"

Lisa shrugged.

Marcus laughed. "I don't know, either. Eddie has somebody else handling my investments now. And I've had some pretty good years in the money department myself. What were we talking about anyway? How'd I get on to this?"

She said, "Wouldn't it be a good idea to call the police and find out what the autopsy showed?"

"It's not going to show anything."

"Please call them, Pops." She smiled at him.

He laughed and shook his head. "Talk about a whim of iron!"

She followed him into his den, where he made the call to the local precinct. She left her pretty drink in the sun room. Marcus was having a tough time getting the information. At one point he said, "Would you prefer to have me call the commissioner?" The menace in his voice surprised Lisa, but apparently it worked.

When he finally hung up he was frowning. "Your grandfather died of a fractured skull," he said.

Lisa gaped at him and burst into tears. "Then—then old Shep—they killed old Shep for nothing!"

He took her in his arms. "Not exactly," he said. "Not the way they see it."

"How stupid can they get, Pops!" she bawled. "Shep could of—" She struggled out of his arms.

"What they think," he said. "They think that the dog—"

"What? What? The dog what? Old Shep picked up a club and hit Gramps over the head with it? Is that what they think? They're all dumb fucking shitepokes, that's what they are!"

27

"Shush a minute, honey. Calm down and I'll tell you what they think. Okay?"

She glared at him with reddened eyes.

"What the lieutenant said was this, I'm only telling you what the lieutenant said. Since there was just Dad and the dog there, and since Dad was a weak old man—"

"He wasn't weak, damn it! He was very strong for his age!"

"For his age," Marcus said quietly. "They say that the only explanation is that Shep charged at Dad, knocked him backward, and Dad hit his head on something hard like the iron piping on the frame of the fencing. That's what the lieutenant said."

Lisa stared at him. "Do you believe that baloney?"

Marcus Honeywell shook his head slowly. "It's hard to picture it happening that way, isn't it?" he said. "But—"

"But what?"

"How else could it have happened?"

"Someone killed him, that's how else! Lemme ask you this, Pops. Did you ever know Gramps to put a dog out in the run that early in the morning, maybe it was still dark, *did you?*"

"No, but Dad was getting forgetful in his old age. It's possible he forgot to take Shep in the night before and left him out all night."

"Sure, and maybe he woke up at six o'clock and remembered—"

"Maybe Shep was barking."

"And Gramps with his lousy hearing heard him, so he pulled on his pants and went down in his bare feet to put him back in his cage. But old Shep thought he was a burglar and attacked—"

"Eddie never trained him as a guard dog. He was just a pet."

Lisa glared at her father. "Can you picture it happening that way?"

Marcus Honeywell shook his head. "No," he said. Then he said, "But—"

Marcus put the phone back in its cradle, and immediately it rang. He grimaced and picked it up. "Eddie! You're back," he said.

Lisa went upstairs to change into her best pair of black jeans, which was her idea of "getting dressed" to go to the Savage Point Steak House, where her father chose to have dinner. She looked at herself in the mirror, saw that the area around her eyes was red and puffy. She curled her lips into an exaggerated sneer, then grinned at her play-acting.

When she returned downstairs, Marcus said, "Eddie Epstein's back. He wants to bury Shep in his backyard."

"Tell him I want to be there for the service," she said.

"Service?"

"You know. Ceremony. Shep deserves a good funeral. Do you think the minister—?"

"You're kidding!"

"Okay, I'll do it myself. How does that thing in the Bible go? 'The Lord is my shepherd, something, something, He makes me lie down in green pastures.' Uncle Eddie's backyard is a green pasture, isn't it? I'll look it up. What hymn could we sing? We need a hymn."

Marcus laughed uncertainly and shook his head. "Listen, your Uncle Eddie said—"

"How about 'You're Nothin' But a Hound Dog?' "

"That's enough, honey. I see you're not interested in what Eddie said about Shep's teeth."

"What about Shep's teeth?"

"He said Shep was so old he had lost most of his teeth."

"How about those two big ones?" she said. "He still had them. I saw them."

"Well, yes, they were about all he had, and they were wobbly. Your grandfather was trying to save them."

"So he couldn't of killed Gramps, right?"

"Looks that way to me."

"That's what I thought," she said solemnly.

Her father gripped her shoulders and turned her toward the staircase. "I thought you were going to get dressed," he said.

"I *am* dressed," she cried.

"You're still wearing jeans."

She replied haughtily, "For your information, they're Gloria Vanderbilt jeans."

He said, "Forgive my ignorance, Princess. If that's it, let's go."

"I'm not hungry."

"Let's go anyway," he said. "By the way, Greg called."

"Why didn't you tell me?" she cried. Greg Muldavin was the closest thing she had to a steady boyfriend.

"He said he didn't want to tie up the phone. He'll drop by later."

They drove in her father's stodgy black Mark VII. Marcus Honeywell would have greatly preferred driving something sportier, like a Ferrari or a Porsche, but as an elected American official he felt he should drive a good old dependable American car. The setting sun was putting on a spectacular light show over the bluffs of Bayside across the water, but neither of them noticed it.

She said, "I think we should stop and say hello to Uncle Shaky."

"Why?"

"He's all alone. Gramps was all he had."

Marcus glanced sideways at her. "And?"

"What do you mean, 'and'?"

"If I know you, honey, you have another reason for seeing Tom Shakespeare."

"Well . . . it does seem to me he's now living in *your* house, not Gramps's, and he may not be able to live there much longer—"

Marcus snorted. "Bull," he said.

They found the large wreck of a man in the dimly lit upstairs sitting room slouched on a sofa, facing an empty overstuffed armchair with permanent indentations from decades of human occupancy. "That was Homer's chair," he muttered.

Marcus turned on the reading lamp near the chair, then sat in it. "We came to see how you're holding up, old man," he said with false heartiness. "We're heading for the steak house, why don't you come with us? No sense sitting here and brooding, it only puts wrinkles on your face."

Shakespeare gave a short laugh. "I'll never get wrinkles, Marc, didn't you know that? I figure if I keep gaining weight steadily, a little at a time, as soon as a wrinkle starts to appear it's filled in with yesterday's potatoes. As Jimmy Durante said of the man on a youthful diet, in my casket I'll look like a baby."

"So come along and get your potatoes."

The old man shook his head and smiled. "Thank you, Marc, but I've already eaten. Franks and beans and a package of Twinkies. So you needn't worry about me, you and my pretty-as-a-picture niece-a Lisa, I'm full of beans, not to mention piss and vinegar. No, you two run along and leave me to my reveries. I'll be all right."

"You were thinking about Gramps, weren't you?" Lisa said.

The old man's face took on a soft internal glow like a Japanese lantern. "The good old days, the bad old days. Yes, your grandfather and I went through a lot together in the old days, little girl. We were pardners, that's what we called ourselves, pardners, from the Zane Grey stories we read and the Western movies we saw. 'Smile when you say that, pardner.' Aah, they don't make movies like that anymore."

"No, they don't," Marcus agreed.

"It only cost a nickel to get in," the old man went on. "Our folks didn't have much money, but we never starved, not until the Great Depression. And when we wanted to act grown-up, we went off in the woods and smoked. There were a lot of woods around then. We'd buy the cigarettes one at a time, 'loosies,' we called them. A penny a cigarette. We could always scrounge up a couple of cents. Aah, you don't want to hear all this."

"What about the Great Depression?" Lisa asked.

"Well, that hit everybody," Shakespeare said. "I was thinking of that just before you came in. There came a time, Homer and I were about twenty, it was around 1930 or '31—we had gotten in a year of college, and then there was no more money. The folks just didn't have any more in the bank, and there were no jobs.

"So Homer and I decided to go West. To seek our fortunes. I don't recall us using those words, but we were young and that notion was in our minds. We also figured it would be more romantic to starve on the range than to starve here. Neither of us had ever shot a gun, but we were gonna shoot deer, live off the meat, and make clothes out of the hides. We were Natty Bumppo and Buffalo Bill put together, and who said we couldn't be. It was every kid's dream."

Lisa said, "Did you go by covered wagon?"

Shakespeare laughed. "No. I'll tell you how we went. We hitchhiked. Your grandfather was the strong, silent type, as they say, and I was the one with the gift of gab, which is how I later came to be an insurance salesman. You need a lot of wind to be an insurance salesman. We were a good team. Homer would somehow get in front of a car—smiling, he had a great smile—and I'd sweet talk the driver into giving us a lift. A neighbor drove us into Manhattan, then we tried to sneak aboard the Weehawken ferry, but we got caught and had to let go of two of our precious nickels. To this day I bear ill will toward that miserable ferry guard.

"Well, to make a dull story duller, we separated in Ohio. I got a job selling, of all things, barber chairs. Yes, barber chairs! It wasn't all that easy. I had to cover three or four states, but I made a few sales, never mind how, you can bet there wasn't much demand for barber chairs in the depth of the Depression.

"Anyhow, Homer left me there, and I didn't see him again for about a year. I got back home before he did, and I got a few sales jobs to keep body and soul together. When Homer got back he was somehow different, which is only natural, I guess. He was quieter than ever, it was hard to get a word out of him, and he seemed downcast. And he had all this money."

"Money?" Marcus said.

"A lot of it, Marc. Didn't he ever tell you about that? I never did know how much it was, but it was a fortune. As I say, he'd gone West to seek his fortune, and, by golly, he found it. But he was acting funny about it. Then after a little while he snapped out of his funk. He said he was going to Cornell and devote the rest of his life to animals, like it was a vocation to the ministry or he was going to Molokai and take care of the lepers.

"And I'll say this, little girl—from that moment on, Homer was the, how shall I say it, the funny, peaceable man you knew as your grandfather. Yes sir, Homer Honeywell was a great man, one of God's noble men."

He struggled to his feet. "Homer liked a rye highball along about this time of night. Would either of you care to join me?"

Lisa watched him move toward the kitchen. It seemed to her that he had lost some mobility in the few hours since morning, and she felt very sad.

When he returned with his drink, he laboriously lowered himself back onto the sofa, sighing.

Marcus said, "So he used some of the money to put himself through Cornell."

"And to set up his business here," Shakespeare said. "But that was it. He handed the rest over to that banker fellow in trust for future heirs."

"That was me," Marcus said.

"Yes."

A few minutes later when they were starting to leave, Shakespeare said, "Don't worry about me and the house here, Marc. I'll find a nice little place to go to, I don't need anything this big—"

"Baloney, Tom," Marcus said. "This is your home, and you're staying here as long as you want. This is your home."

The old man nodded. "We'll see," he said.

At the door, Lisa said, "How far did Gramps get?"

"What?"

"Did my grandfather say how far he had gotten when he went West?"

"Oh, he got to California. Do you know I've never been west of Chicago, and he got to California."

"What did he do there? Did he say?"

The old man shook his head. "All he told me was that he had worked on a sheep ranch. Maybe that's where he got his love for animals."

They left him sitting on the sofa with a rye highball in his hand, facing an empty easy chair.

They were driving down Marathon Parkway when Marcus Honeywell said to his daughter, "Well, I'll be a monkey's uncle, I do believe we're being followed."

Lisa looked back. "It's the security patrol car," she said. "Probably Paulie."

"Isn't he off his beat?"

Lisa yawned. "He doesn't care. He likes to follow me."

"He does this often?"

"He and Brucie, they think it's funny."

Marcus pulled the car to the side of the road. "Well, I'm giving him a cease-and-desist order right now."

She said, "Let it go, Pops. I can always lose him when I want to. He's not doing any harm."

"You sure?"

"Sure."

"I don't like it."

The security patrol car passed the Mark VII and turned onto the expressway service road.

"It was Paulie," Lisa said. "Let's go, Pops."

"I still don't like it," her father said, frowning.

Four

WHEN GREG MULDAVIN held Lisa in his arms, his chin rested on top of her head, and when she put her arms around his spare frame, she had the impression she could wrap them twice around. They stood on the sea wall across Shore Road from Lisa's house, two swaying figures in the soft night.

"Relax, sweetie," he said.

"I am," she mumbled into his dungaree jacket. "I'm falling asleep right now."

"*Au contraire, ma chérie,*" he said, utilizing what little French he had learned in high school. "You're wound up so tight you're about to go spinning off into space like one of those gyro toys."

She giggled at the image of her whirling out of his arms and up into the stars.

Dinner at the Steak House had been a disaster. First, her stomach was rebelling at the thought of food and she was rebelling against her father for insisting on taking her there. She said all she wanted was franks and beans. He said the Steak House didn't serve franks and beans and suggested a nice T-bone medium rare. She made retching sounds. They glared at each other. He said, Okay, order what you want. She ordered a double serving of vanilla ice cream. He reacted as expected, and she asked him sweetly why dessert always had to come last when you had no room left, why shouldn't you have it first when it tasted so good. He threw his hands in the air and said, Have it your own way.

Then the people started coming to the table. The Savage Point Steak House was one of Marcus Honeywell's regular ports of call where his wealthier constituents spoke quietly to him of their concerns. They amused him because he knew that their concept of government was one whose sole function was to maintain an efficient police force to protect them from criminals, civic planners, ecologists, abortionists, militant atheists, and other un-American elements. This evening they came to commiserate over his father's death—a social amenity, don't you know—and incidentally to mention what was really on their minds: the threat of low-cost housing, tighter gun control, installation of sanitary sewers, and drug abuse by teenagers.

The whole Webster family was there, an unusual occurrence in recent years since twenty-two-year-old Bruce generally preferred the company of his own gang of peers. Meg was the only Webster who came to the Honeywell table. The plump young woman gave Lisa a quick hug, expressed her sympathy, and whispered that she'd see Lisa the next day.

The parents, Malcolm and Eunice, sat like benevolent wax figures from the Edwardian era. Benevolent, that is, until it came to the person of Marcus Honeywell. To them, Marcus was a dangerous man, a Communist sympathizer if not an out-and-out Red. Unfortunately they were tied to him, for Malcolm's father, old Angus Webster, in his dotage had made the brilliant young lawyer, Marcus Honeywell, executor and trustee of the family estate. Several years ago they had petitioned the surrogate's court to switch the trusteeship to a more compatible person, but by that time his custodianship had effected a fifty-percent increase in the corpus of the trust, and the kindly surrogate had advised the Websters to withdraw their petition. Marcus's secret of success was simplicity itself—listen closely to Eddie Epstein's investment counselor and follow his advice.

Between interruptions at the table Lisa fixed an empty gaze on the Websters while her mind tossed and turned, unable to rest. The mother's face was powdered and her eyes were too small, like two raisins in a ball of dough. The father's handsome, decaying face had a dull sheen as if coated with the pomade that slicked down his iron-gray hair. Lisa's friend Meg was still young enough to look at everything and everyone around her with a measure of eagerness made tentative by the fear of rebuff. Bruce was the only one who didn't look as if he were bursting with health. There was a gauntness and yet a suggestion of slackness in his pale face that made him look much older than his years.

Lisa switched her gaze to her own father and grinned, thinking that, as fathers went, hers was the best and she was lucky to have chosen him. He knew how to have fun, even while he was bamboozling these self-anointed sachems of local society with his charm.

Jack Doran, the garden man, was there. Though he provided green-thumb services for many of the residents, his breezy facade and expansive Texas accent—and his apparent financial success—made him acceptable as an equal. Despite his Irish name, Lisa thought that his straight black hair and leathery complexion hinted at Mexican blood in his heritage.

Tonight he was dressed as usual in a white shirt, blue blazer, and gray slacks. Lisa thought of it as his uniform. She had never seen him dressed in any other way—a landlocked yachtsman in a boating community.

Standing over them, he touched their shoulders lightly with his hands. "Ah'm sorry about the ole doc," he said. "We all are gonna miss the ole gent, and that's for sure."

Marcus solemnly thanked him.

"If there's anythin' Ah can do—"

Marcus said, "Yes, there is, Jack. I hear you go back every year to Texas to renew your accent. Don't do it this year, I beg you. Hell, as it is, I need subtitles half the time to understand what you all are saying."

Doran laughed excessively and clapped Marcus on the shoulder. That laugh put the final twist on Lisa's string of nerves . . .

She spun out of Greg's arms on the sea wall in imitation of a whirling toy, and Greg had to catch her before she spiraled off the edge into the rocks below.

"Dummy," he said. "I didn't mean for you to do it."

In clutching at him, her hand touched a leather scabbard attached to his belt. "What's that?" she asked.

"What's what?"

"This."

"Oh, that. I was going to show you, but I didn't think it was the right time."

In the semidarkness she could see the small smile on his face showing pride of possession. "It's a monster," she said.

He carefully extracted the large knife from its sheath and placed it in her hands. "Careful," he said.

Gingerly she touched the razor-sharp edges of the blade, the saw teeth, the pointed projections on the hilt guard. "It's hoo-mungous," she said.

"Isn't it a beauty?" he said. "It's an all-purpose knife for scuba divers. The blade and teeth can cut through anything, and if you tie a line here, you can use it as a grappling hook."

"So when are you going scuba diving?"

"You don't have to go diving, dummy. I use it every day when I'm working for Mr. Doran. I could cut down a tree with it, or draw a pint of blood faster than the Red Cross."

"Ugh," she said, handing back the knife.

"I mean it," he said. "If someone killed your grandfather, let's find out who it was. Don't do anything dopey yourself, let me handle it."

There was a braggadocio in Greg that disturbed her. He had always been interested in weapons, perhaps because he had been painfully thin as a child and hence the butt of some cruel jokes. No one made fun of him any more now that he was tall and strong, but the insecurity remained. He had dreamed of going to West Point or Annapolis, but his school marks just weren't good enough and he had wound up going to the Merchant Marine Academy on King's Point, where he was now in his second year.

She said, "If anyone's going to handle it, it's going to be the police. I don't want you killing someone and saying, Oop, sorry, wrong one. That's what you'd do, I know it."

"Aw, come on," he said in a hurt tone.

Instantly contrite, she said, "I'm sorry, Greg, I didn't mean that." And she kissed him.

She was alone in the big house. At ten-thirty her father had said, "I have to go over a few things with Eddie Epstein. Don't wait up for me. Go to bed and get a good night's sleep, you're going to need it, honey." He hugged her and said, "Are you going to be all right?"

"Sure, Pops, no problem. Give Uncle Eddie a kiss for me."

Marcus Honeywell laughed uncertainly and left.

Lisa knew where he was going, and the kiss wasn't going to be delivered to Epstein. She knew the symptoms. Ever since they had returned from the restaurant he had been more restless than usual. He had gone into his den and sat at his desk. He lasted there five minutes. Then he had gone to the sun room and stared out at the dark water. Four minutes. He had inspected the dust on the piano and made a comment about the day maids. Thirty seconds. That sort of thing.

No, Marcus Honeywell was going to see the only person who could calm him down—Mathilde Raymond. Mrs. Raymond was the secretary in his law office, a pleasant, plumpish woman of forty who had taken on the extra-legal duties of ministering to Marcus Honeywell's personal needs some time after Lisa's mother had deserted ship four years ago. Long separated from a drunken husband, she performed both roles, secretarial and romantic, with serene efficiency.

Marcus was as discreet as he could be, which wasn't very discreet given his high visibility; he believed that his regular visits to her apartment in Bayside either went unnoticed or were attributed to late-night work, legal and legislative. Unfortunately, one who did notice was Mathilde's barfly husband who loitered in the vicinity night after night like a wolf whose lair has been destroyed.

Lisa had observed the finale of the man's bungled attempt at blackmail. She was approaching her father's storefront office on Northern Boulevard when the man came pinwheeling out and slammed against a parked car. Marcus, standing in the doorway, called sweetly, "Bye-bye, Charles."

The rumpled man, holding a handkerchief to his nose, spoke the time-honored words, "You'll be sorry for this, Honeywell."

That was a year ago, and, as far as Lisa knew, the man had done nothing to cause Marcus to be sorry.

Or had he?

She tried to imagine Charles Raymond getting back at Marcus by killing Marcus's father and immediately shook her head at the implausibility of it. No way, she thought, no way could the drunken derelict have carried out the deception of the mangled throat. True, it was in character for the man who has a grudge against someone he can't harm directly to go after a vulnerable person close to him. She pictured Charles Raymond attacking her grandfather—and saw her grandfather, despite his seventy-five years, kicking the floundering man out of the office!

How Mathilde could have married the man in the first place, Lisa didn't know. Marriage was a game of blind man's bluff. You clutched at someone in the dark and were supposed to be stuck with him for the rest of your life. What a system! Look at Marcus and her mother.

Blooey. Look at Mathilde. Blooey. Look at the Websters. Who'd want to marry him? Imagine being in bed with him. Yuk. She and Greg took care of the sex part pretty well. Since her father was away most of the week, she had the house to herself, so there was no need to rush into any lifelong commitment. What sort of husband would Greg Muldavin make? No need to find out yet, thank God. Play it day to day.

She got a glass of milk and a box of Mallomars from the kitchen and took them up to her bedroom. Her nightdress consisted of a pair of panties and one of her father's old shirts. Tuning her color TV to a "M°A°S°H" rerun, she propped herself on the bed and slowly munched on the marshmallow cookies. The sound on the TV was set so low that she could listen or not, as she wished; she knew most of the episodes by heart anyway. After "M°A°S°H" would come a rerun of "The Honeymooners" and then "The Rookies." This was her lair, her retreat to security.

Her responsible self wondered if she had locked the downstairs doors and windows, but her happy-go-lucky self said, Why worry.

Now she could let her grandfather enter her thoughts. He had been so much a part of her that the sudden loss was like an amputation. Lolling against the pillows now was like cuddling in his lap and listening to his stories—stories according to Homer. All of them were about animals, real animals like dogs, cats, raccoons, chipmunks, cows, sheep, lions, and tigers; and fabulous animals of his own invention, like the rhinopotamus who got so fat he floated into the air, and everyone thought he was a blimp until he defecated in midair and plugged up a Mexican volcano that was about to erupt, thus saving the living creatures for miles around. He called the volcano "Po-po-cat-a-petal," which Lisa thought was very funny. His humor tended to be scatalogical. Sometimes he fell asleep before she did—or pretended to—and then she would give him a butterfly kiss on his cheek or blow in his ear until he would wake up with an exaggerated jump.

He read to her too, starting with nursery rhymes in which he substituted Lisa's name for the name in the rhyme. One of her favorites was:

> *Lisa had a little lamb,*
> *Its fleece was white as snow,*
> *And everywhere that Lisa went*
> *The lamb was sure to go.*

Later he tried to read some more mature stories to her, but by then she had discovered television and become an addict despite the rantings of her parents. It was so much easier than trying to read. Still she remained Grampa's girl. She snuggled into the pillows . . .

The only article of clothing Marcus Honeywell kept at Mathilde's apartment was a plain cotton robe with light blue stripes that was neither male nor female in gender, a unisex garment that blended well enough with the other garments in her closet. He wore it now as he lay sprawled on her sofa, temporarily at ease.

The two observed certain conventions peculiar to themselves. One of them was that civilized persons did not parade around in the nude and would never think of depositing one's moist skin on upholstered furniture. And his skin was now decidedly moist.

Mathilde Raymond was well proportioned in the classical sense rather than the Hollywood starlet sense. In the office, with her chestnut hair pulled back and her hazel eyes framed by rimless glasses, she was an imposing figure. Now with her hair loosened and her glasses resting on her bedside table and clothed in a ruffled peignoir of evening-gown length, she was the gracious hostess serving her companion a steaming cup of hot chocolate.

"This will calm the cockles," she said.

He said, "Can't stay too long, love. Gotta get back."

"Surely she's asleep by now," she said, moving her knitting basket and sitting beside him on the sofa, without touching.

"Even so," he said.

He picked up the cup, then placed it back down on the coffee table. "What was the name of that play?" he said. "*I Never Sang For My Father*? Shit, I never did anything for him! I never tap-danced or juggled or even hugged him. We always shook hands, like he was my uncle or just a friend I'd bump into every once in a while. You know, Hi, friend, how are you, you're looking good, oops, gotta go, bye. What a son! What a son of a bitch! Thinking only of myself—"

"He didn't *want* anything from you, Marc," she said. "Just for you to be someone he could be proud of, that was all. You're a good man, a fine lawyer, a prominent—"

He grunted in self-derision. "A phony-baloney politician! You know what he really wanted me to be? A veterinarian! I was in my third year at Cornell when I came into that dough. I was taking prevet courses, then I switched to law without telling him.

"Do you know what did it? I was in the dissecting room, it was a big cement area, and there was this horse lying there with these miles and miles of bloody bluish intestines snaking around the room, and I stood there with blood on my shoes, and I said, Who needs this? This is obscene!

"It didn't go with the image I had of myself. I didn't want to be my father, I wanted to be me. I was above poking around in dead intestines. I wanted to ride horses, not rip them open. And suddenly I was independent. I could do what I wanted, and the hell with my father! The money did that, the money he set up for me. If it weren't for the blasted money I'd probably have become a veterinarian, and he would have been happy."

"But would you?"

"Would I what?"

"Would you have been happy as a vet?"

"Oh, I suppose so. But it would have been a business, not a calling the way it was for Dad."

"I'm sure he knew that," she said. "Drink your hot chocolate, Marc. It takes the sting out of regret."

He drank some of the thick fluid, then planted a chocolate kiss on her neck, and shortly afterward they adjourned once again to the bedroom for some more of "Doctor" Raymond's physical therapy, a slower, longer, sweeter passage of two bodies in tune.

He was on the verge of sleep when the phone rang, and Mathilde answered it. She said, "Oh, for God's sake!" Then she said, "Knock it off, Charles," and slammed down the phone.

He said fuzzily, "What was that?"

She said, "Heavy breathing. I could almost smell the whiskey fumes."

"Does he do this often?"

"No. Don't worry about it, Marc. He's a terrible pest, but he's harmless."

Marcus sat up. "Good legal point. Can heavy breathing be considered an obscene phone call? Maybe the person has asthma or had just run in a marathon. No, heavy breathing is not per se obscene. But it *is* harassment. Let's slap an injunction on the bastard."

"Marc," she said firmly. "Let it be. Neither of us wants the publicity, do we?"

A few minutes later, Marcus Honeywell got out of Mathilde Raymond's bed and languidly put on his clothes. She watched him. There was a melancholy in her eyes.

The television set was still on. The sound woke Lisa, and she peered blearily at the set. A man and a woman were in bed coming on heavy, as if they were really making it. They seemed to be eating each other's face. But the sound didn't go with the love-making. It was a high screech. Lisa thought, Rats, the set is broken. She found the remote control gadget and switched it off. But the screech continued.

She licked melted chocolate from her fingers while she pondered the source of the noise . . .

One of the smoke alarms!

She scrambled from the bed and ran downstairs. A sharp metallic odor stung her nostrils. The screech was coming from the kitchen. She pushed open the door, and black smoke hit her in the face. She plunged through it to the stove, saw with astonishment not only that the deep-fry pot filled with oil was perched there but that the oil was on fire and that the pot was melting. The oil fire was blue. The flames that licked the sides of the pot from the gas burner beneath it were yellow and orange. She tried to turn off the jet, but the control knob was sizzling and seemed to be stuck in the open position. Using a hot-pot holder, she managed to turn it off.

She was gagging, the alarm was screeching and the oil was still on fire. A blob of molten aluminum fell from the bottom of the pot onto the red hot burner. A cover. She needed a cover to smother the flame! Her eyes were tearing, so that she couldn't see. Crouching on hands and knees, she crept to the cabinet where the pots were stored, blindly reached in, and found a cover that was large enough.

She stood by the stove. The top of the burning pot listed to one side. She had to be very, very careful. If she didn't place the cover on it just right, the cover would slide, topple the pot, and splash the flaming liquid all over her and the rest of the kitchen. She slowly lowered the pot lid so that its curved lip held it in place, and the flame went out.

Then she was down on the floor again, crawling to the doors and windows, opening them wide. After doing that, she went to the sink and vomited.

Marcus Honeywell arrived home at two o'clock. He was surprised to find the lights on and Lisa moving about in her version of the baby-doll nightie, an outraged look on her baby-doll face.

She took him by the hand, said, "Come here, Pops," and led him to the blackened kitchen.

He said, "What in God's name did you do, honey?"

"Nothing," she said huskily. "I was asleep. Someone tried to burn the house down."

"Oh, Lisa!" he said with a groan of disbelief. He strode to the stove, glared at the misshapen pot that looked like it has been designed by Salvador Dali.

"Don't touch it," she said. "You'll lose your hand."

He said, "Somebody left the burner on." He turned and frowned at her.

"Somebody *turned* it on, Pops."

Not hearing her, he said, "What were you doing, making french fries? You didn't eat a thing at the restaurant. No wonder you were hungry."

"Don't be a thick-headed shitepoke, Pops!" she shouted. "I didn't turn it on! I had some Mallomars and milk, that's all!"

What Lisa was suggesting was too unbelievable. He peered around uncertainly. "There's nothing to be done right now. That burner's ruined. It'll have to be replaced. Come on, let's get out of here."

They moved out into the front hall. He said, "You don't suppose Brenda or Cobina could have left the pot on the stove?" He was referring to their two day maids.

"Pops," she said. "Pops, listen. You were in the kitchen before we went out to eat. Was that pot on the stove?"

He frowned. "Not that I noticed."

"It wasn't, believe me," she said. "I have good eyes, right? You always said so. I went into the kitchen to get my snack. The burner was off. The pot was *not* on the stove. The maids didn't do it, and I didn't do it. Either somebody else did it, or we have ghosts."

"You sure?"

"Sure I'm sure."

He broke off eye contact. "Sure stinks in here," he said. Something on the hall table near the front door caught his eye. "What are my kid gloves doing here? I haven't worn them in months."

She said, "Never mind the gloves, Pops, what are we going to do? Somebody tried to burn the house down."

Marcus Honeywell embraced his daughter. His mind was dulled by fatigue. "First, we're going to make sure that the windows and doors are locked," he said. "Then we're going to sleep on it. There must be some explanation."

"Yes, father," she said in a flat voice.

At five in the morning a black-clad figure stole into Mathilde Raymond's bedroom hit her on the head with a metal bar, then with surgical precision inserted her steel knitting needles into her heart. Attached to the needles were a half-finished blouse and a ball of wool yarn, which fell to the floor and rolled halfway across the room.

Eddie Epstein found her at eleven. Unable to rouse her by phone, he had gone to her apartment and persuaded the superintendent to open her door.

Marcus Honeywell came a short time later. He fell apart, spoke irrationally, and shuddered uncontrollably until Epstein gripped Marcus's shoulders painfully hard.

Lisa came and drove her father home.

Then she went to Greaney's Funeral Home and picked out a casket for her grandfather. Since there wasn't a plain pine one available, she chose the most expensive, on the theory that since they were all too grand she and her father might as well send the old veterinarian off in the Cadillac of caskets. "Far out," she said.

Then she went back home and listened to her father's grief. The disjointed monologue lasted all afternoon. She had never felt closer to him in her life.

Five

THE TWO WAKES were held at the same funeral home in adjoining parlors. Bill Greaney was sincerely embarrassed at Marcus Honeywell's double bereavement. "Who needs this, I don't need this," he moaned to Marcus. "I certainly don't."

"Neither do I," Marcus said.

Marcus conducted himself with dignity and sad serenity. Only the occasional tremor in his hands and voice betrayed his inner tension. The newspaper accounts identified him merely as Mathilde Raymond's employer, but his secret was out. Nobody believed he was in her apartment until two A.M. to discuss business or perhaps to say a "Pater Noster," although not a soul brought it up to his face—except, of course, the righteous Malcolm Webster.

"I want you to resign from the trust," Webster said bluntly.

Marcus bowed. "It was very thoughtful of you to

come and pay your respects to my father," he said. "Are you an animal lover, Malcolm?"

They were standing in the hall outside the adjoining parlors. Webster glanced around uneasily. "I suppose this isn't the place, is it?" he said. "I'm sorry about your—about your—"

"You were talking about the trust."

"It can wait."

"Why should I resign, Malcolm?"

"Well now, I'm sure you agree that a trustee is in a position of—well, of trust," Webster said, truculent yet ill at ease. "And when a question of moral turpitude rises to destroy that fragile bond of trust and casts doubt on the, er, probity of the, er, trustee—"

"Is there something wrong with the way I've handled the investments?"

"Well, no, but that has nothing to do with it."

"It has everything to do with it," Marcus said in the same quiet voice he had used throughout the exchange.

"Not completely," Webster said. "Not completely. I'm sure the surrogate will not wish to condone adultery in—"

"I'm sure he wouldn't," Marcus said. "But I think he would tell you that my private life is my own affair and has nothing to do with my custodianship of the Webster trust. Now, if you'll excuse me." Marcus moved away to chat glumly with new arrivals.

Lisa watched him, marveling at his control. In her mind she was not only watching him but watching *over* him, determined to protect him from a lurking killer who seemed to be circling her father. She was not unaware that she was part of the circle and might herself be the next target, as she was sure she had been in the kitchen episode. But being young and healthy she put little credence in the possibility of her own death. No, her father, who was more than twice her age, was the one who needed protection.

She responded mechanically and with her father's dignity to those who came with brimming eyes to clasp her hand and embrace her. For the first time in her life she felt dislodged from the stable world of childhood, adrift in unknown, and therefore frightening, currents. Meg Webster stayed close to her, saying little, an inert presence, a lumpy duffel bag, so to speak, containing a jumble of mementos, confidences, and playthings from the safe world that was now gone. Someone to mutter things to without need for a response.

"Thank you very much, Mr. Doran. Yes, a sad occasion. What's that? Well, maybe not a saint exactly, but yes, a good man. Thank you . . . *What a cotton-pickin' phony! He didn't care a shit about Gramps and now he's making him out to be a saint! He's so full of fertilizer I can smell the poo-ey manure* . . . I get the message, Brucie, you don't have to say anything. So how are things at Berkeley . . .? That's a long way to go just to flunk out. I'm sure it was fun, if you say so. No, I wouldn't have lasted this long. So what are your plans now? Well, you'll come up with something. No, I never heard of Hate Ashberry, who's Ashberry? Oh. Well, take care, Brucie . . . *I don't care if he is your brother, he gives me the willies. It's like he went off on a trip and never came back. How can you live with him . . .?*"

And so on.

When Eddie Epstein embraced her, she nearly broke down. He was a muscular man close to six feet tall, with crinkled reddish hair and a craggy face. He was dressed in dark brown slacks and a tweed jacket with leather patches at the elbows.

"Be good to that father of yours," he said. "He needs you now, Lisa. This thing has knocked him for a loop."

"I will, Uncle Eddie," she said. "I'm sorry about Shep."

"Oh, well, he was an old dog. He had his day. Still, I'm going to miss him."

"My father said you were going to bury him in the backyard."

"Already did. Over by the old hydrangea. I cried all the time."

"I wanted to be there."

"We'll have a ceremony when we put up a headstone. I'll call you."

"Okay."

They were silent for a minute.

"You were out of town," she said.

"Yes. I wish I had stayed there." He sighed heavily. "But then it would have been Marcus who found Mathilde. I couldn't wish that on him."

"Do you have to go back?"

"No, I think I can handle the rest of the paperwork from here. I was going to take a few extra days just to look around. I'd never been to California before. Oh well, what the hell."

"Where were you?"

"San Francisco. What I saw of it made me want to see more. But—"

"Who did it, Uncle Eddie?"

"Did what?"

"Killed Mrs. Raymond."

He let his shoulders slump. "I don't know, sweetie. The police think it might have been her husband, but I don't know. It was a screwy way to kill someone, almost as if it were a part of a ritual."

"Just like Gramps," Lisa said.

Epstein stepped back and peered at her quizzically.

"Oh, yes," Lisa said, nodding emphatically. "He was murdered. And I'm going to find out who, and I'm going to rip his throat out the way he did to Gramps. I'm going to break his head, and then I'm going to take a knife or something—I saw on TV those things they use on the docks, those sharp hooks, and that's what I'm going to use to make it look like a dog did it, but first I'll tie him and then wake him up so he can watch what I'm doing to his throat, and I'll spit in his eyes—"

Epstein reached for her and pressed her face against his chest. "I get the picture, Lisa," he growled. "So do me a favor. Forget about it for now. Your father needs you, and he doesn't need you talking crazy. Go stand near him, okay? Be his interference, block out some of those wailing witches before they drive him batty." He moved her back from him and said, "Now let me see a smile."

She put on a phony imitation of a smile. "I know what," she said. "I'll get down behind their knees, and he can shove them over me. How's that?"

"Perfect," Epstein said.

Nearly all of the mourners were there to pay their respects to Old Doc Honeywell. Mathilde Raymond had no close relatives on the East Coast. Those who came to mourn her, aside from Marcus and Eddie, were Bayside neighbors and the "M and M girls," her three middle-aged bridge partners, all of whom had names beginning with M—Marilyn, Maisie, and Miriam.

And then there was Charles Raymond.

Lisa saw him first. He stood just inside the outside door, hang-dog and defiant, dressed in an ill-matching blue serge jacket and tan trousers. The jacket was obviously not a separate but the remnant of a suit, the trousers of which had worn out. His slightly bloated face was clean-shaven, and his black hair was slicked down. All dressed up for a funeral.

Lisa nudged her father, and felt him stiffen. The surprise was that Charles Raymond was there at all. The last Lisa had heard was that the pitiful man was being detained by the police for questioning. His freedom to attend Mathilde's wake indicated either that he had satisfied the police of his noncomplicity in her murder, or that they had no evidence against him other than his relationship to her.

Lisa said to her father, "Let's get some air. I'm getting close to phobia."

"Claustrophobia," he said, idly correcting her. He followed her out the side door to the cool parking lot.

They leaned against a parked car.

He said, "When I go, honey, don't hold one of these. Just get Jack Doran's crew to dig a hole in the yard—"

"Sure, Pops."

"And have them bury me sitting up, with my head above ground facing the bay. I always liked the view."

She didn't reply.

"That's not very funny, is it?" he said.

"You're not going, Pops," she said. "Tell me about Mrs. Raymond."

"What do you want to know?"

"About her and that goonybird. How come she ever tied up with him?"

Marcus Honeywell sighed. "I don't know, honey. All I know is people change. Would you believe Charles Raymond was a high-school football star? That's what Mathilde once told me. She didn't know it was going to be the high point of his life. She was very young and they got married, and then—I don't know. Maybe he never grew up. She married a boy who couldn't be a man, is my guess. He worked in a bank at one time, I know that, and Mathilde paid off the bonding company for the money he secretly borrowed and never paid back. You can't be too hard on the poor bastard. Alcoholism is a disease, did you know that?"

"Like drugs."

"So there you are," he said dully. "She finally left him and ran as far from him as she could, from one coast to the other."

"From the West Coast?"

"California, I think," he said. "And he followed her."

Lisa thought for a while, and said, "That's sad."

"A goddamn soap opera," he said.

"Do you think he killed her?"

"If he did, he killed the goose that laid the golden egg. She was supporting him, at least partially. She gave him handouts on demand. It had become a routine. He'd show up, she'd shove the money at him, and he'd go. No spoken demand, no sermon, two minutes, and out. Wham, bam, no thank-you-ma'am."

"She was a kook to do it," Lisa said. "I'd of smashed him in the face and told him to get lost."

Marcus glanced at his daughter with amused eyes. "You're a hard-hearted lady, Miss Honeywell," he said.

"I'd of done it," she assured him. "I would!" Then she realized that her father was smiling for the first time in three days and that her tough talk had momentarily broken his tension. "And if he came back," she went on, "I'd of kicked him in the crotch and—and—"

But Marcus was no longer amused. "We'd better get back in, honey," he said. "After all, it's our party."

She said, "Pops, you're as funny as a bloody nose."

They went back indoors arm in arm, smiling.

Tom Shakespeare sat on a camp chair near the casket of his old friend Homer Honeywell, dangerously overflowing on each side. His face had the pasty look of the dead, and the juxtaposition of his unhealthy carcass to the closed casket—closed because of the dead man's ravaged throat—it was almost as if the corpse was attending its own wake. The sight brought tears to Lisa's eyes.

She sat next to him and said brightly, "How ya doing, Uncle Shaky?"

The voice came faintly from deep inside him. "I've had better days, sweetheart. Lovely casket, isn't it?"

"Nothing but the best for Gramps," she said, shocked at hearing the snarl in her own voice. She hadn't known it was there.

The smell of flowers became sickening and would forever after be the odor of death in her mind.

She returned to her father's side, and became aware of Charles Raymond standing in the doorway to Mathilde's room, his scowling eyes riveted on Marcus Honeywell.

Marcus muttered a barely audible curse and went to the glaring figure. Lisa followed.

Marcus said, "Do you have something to say to me, Mr. Raymond?"

The man took a step backward and bumped against the frame of the doorway. "Any other man would be in jail by now," he said, his voice thick with animosity. "Do they have separate laws for millionaires? Or is it because you're a politician, is that it?"

Marcus said, "Oh, shit, Raymond, I didn't kill Mathilde, and you know it. You were watching, weren't you?"

"Damn right I was watching," the man said. "I've had my eye on you two all along."

Marcus nodded. "Then you know I left her at two o'clock."

"Yes, I know that, your honorable sir. And I saw you come back at five! I saw you go in the window, and I saw you leave the same way. I told the police all this, but you got them buffaloed, haven't you? Why haven't they arrested you, answer me that!"

"Because the police know I have a key," Marcus said. "And because you were drunk. If you were there at five, which I doubt, you were probably in a stupor and didn't see anything."

"Chapter and verse," the man said, his voice rising. "I gave them chapter and verse. You were dressed in black, you came close to where I was sitting. You had on a ski mask, but you couldn't fool me. I saw it was you, you murdering bastard. Then you went up the fire escape and into her window. I told the police all that—"

Marcus interrupted him. "Keep it down, this is a place of mourning. But tell me one thing, how could you recognize me if I was wearing a ski mask?"

"That's what the police wanted to know," Raymond said, dancing with excitement. "I've been watching you a long time, Honeywell, and I know your shape in the dark. But what nailed it down—you want to know how

I recognized you in a ski mask? I'll tell you, it was the ski mask itself! It has a funny pattern of orange and blue, *and it's yours!* I saw you with it last winter when you and the little missy went skating in Harper's Cove. It's yours, Honeywell. There isn't another one like it in the world. And you wore it to—to—" A sob stopped the flow of words.

Lisa remembered the mask. It had been knitted for her grandfather by the Cat Woman; and the old man, who had no use for it, gave it to Marcus. She remembered telling Marcus that it made his head look like an Easter egg, and Marcus had nodded and said, "That's good, I'll wear it."

He now said, "I assure you, Raymond, I didn't kill Mathilde, and that's the end of that." He turned away.

"It's not the end," the man called after him. "Maybe you can get away from the police, but not from God. God'll get you!"

Marcus bumped blindly into Jack Doran, and mumbled, "Sorry."

Doran put a hand on Marcus's shoulder. "Don't worry about it," he said. "The man's a raving loonybird."

"You heard what he said?" Marcus asked.

"Hell, everybody in the hall heard him. The man's obviously unbalanced. It's a dang shame it had to happen here."

Marcus mumbled thanks for his sympathy, and broke away.

Lisa's senses were fogged over. She reacted dully to the remnant of mourners, and when visiting hours were over, she drove Tom Shakespeare home in her Firebird. She was aware that the security patrol car was following her, and, rather than feeling annoyed, took comfort in the fact that Paul Doran was watching over her. Her father was driving his own car directly home, and Lisa knew he wanted to check the whereabouts of his ski mask.

She had difficulty hoisting Shakespeare out of her low-slung car, and Paul Doran came forward to help her.

"Thank you, children," the bulky man said. "I didn't know these newfangled cars had basements."

They saw him into the house that still displayed the sign: "ANIMAL HOSPITAL, Homer Honeywell, D.V.S."

When she finally got to her own home on Shore Road, she parked in the driveway behind her father's Mark VII. Greg Muldavin was there waiting for her in the dark. He took her in his arms, and she wrapped her arms around him like a child enfolding her favorite teddy bear, with a sense of home and safety and warmth and love. Love? She wanted to think about that. Up until now she and Greg had been pals, who used each other almost casually for emotional explorations rather like two beginners on a ski slope learning the thrills and satisfactions of the sport as they went further and further into the mysteries of each others' hills and valleys and free-gliding zones.

"I'm pooped," she said into his chest. "My rear end is dragging."

"I'll hold it up," he said, and he did.

"Everybody was there. It was murder."

"I know."

"I didn't see you there."

"I was out on the sidewalk."

She pulled away from him. "Why didn't you come in?"

"It's not my scene," he said.

"What do you mean, it's not your scene?"

"I don't like to look at dead bodies, okay?"

"The casket was closed."

"I don't like to look at caskets, either. Come on, I want to show you something." He pulled her down the drive, across Shore Road to the sea wall. They sat on top of the wall with their legs dangling. She shivered in the damp breeze but wouldn't let him put his arm around her.

"I have to go in and be with my father," she said.

"Listen," he said. He paused dramatically. "I think I know what they used on your grandfather!"

She stared at him.

"Mostly Doran's crews do lawns, right?" he said. "But some of the older characters want us to do their gardens, too. And what do you suppose is one of the tools we use?"

His hands were behind his back.

"Come on, Greg, what?"

He whipped his hand from behind him and held a pronged implement an inch from her face. "The *claw*!" he cried, chortling like a comic villain.

She pushed his hand away. "Stop futzing around, damn it," she said. "What is it?"

He hung his head at her rebuke. She saw that what he held was a vicious-looking instrument with three long prongs bent in the shape of a claw, each prong coming to a sharp point. He said, "It's called a cultivator. You see, what you do is dig into a flowerbed and—"

"Lemme see it." She held it in her hands, touched the prongs. "The points are sharp, but there are no cutting edges. I don't see how—"

"Don't you think it would be easy to put an edge on those babies?" he cried. "You wouldn't even need a grindstone—"

"But this has no sharp edges."

"Oh, shit, Lisa, I didn't say that *this* was the weapon, but one *like* it that's been sharpened! It could be done with a file—"

"Who has it?"

"Who has what?"

"The sharpened one."

He took the tool from her and stood up. "I see you're in one of your moods," he said. "Sometimes you act so dumb—forget what I said. Go on in to your father, I'm going home."

She stood up. "It's possible you're right, Gregory," she said. "All I want to know is who."

He stopped at the edge of Shore Road. "There must be fifty or a hundred people in Savage Point who bought one thinking they'd use it. This one was in Doran's truck. God knows how we'd get a look at the others—"

She stretched and kissed him on the lips. She closed her eyes and concentrated on what the kiss was doing to her. Not much. He wasn't responding. The test of love would have to await another time.

She said, "Don't get mad just because I'm dumber than you are. I can't help it."

"Aw, I didn't say that," he protested.

She tugged at him. "Come on, I know where we can check out one of those things right now."

She led him past the cars to the garage, flipped on the interior light. Against the back wall were the gardening utensils on a wooden counter and hanging from a pegboard. Her father hadn't used them in years.

The cultivator hung from a hook on the pegboard. The prongs glinted in the light.

Greg reached for it, and she said, "Don't touch."

He said in an awed voice, "That sucker's been sharpened!"

Lisa felt sick to her stomach. She pulled Greg out of the garage, flicked off the light, and closed the door. She leaned back against the closed door, then pushed herself away from it as if it were too hot to touch.

"Go home," she told Greg. "I'll have my father call the cops in the morning."

Two minutes later she went into the house.

Her father was in the sun room with a drink in one hand and the ski mask in the other. He raised his eyes to her.

"It wasn't in with the winter stuff," he said in a monotone. "It was thrown on the floor of the closet."

Lisa wasn't surprised. She was beyond surprise.

He said, "Someone seems to have the run of the house."

She dropped into the chair opposite his. She needed someone to hug, but her father's position made him inaccessible. She felt cold and alone.

Six

THE DAY AFTER the second funeral Marcus Honeywell slept late, then permitted Eddie Epstein to plunge him into legal work that had been neglected as a result of the deaths. Marcus didn't want to leave Lisa alone, but she said, "Go ahead, Pops, I'm going back to work, too. If I mope around here one more day, they'll have to take me away in a straitjacket." So Marcus went off with Epstein.

Lisa arrived at Roosevelt Field, parked her Firebird, and remained seated behind the wheel. The late June sun baked the acres of cars, and she had the illusion they were melting like snow sculptures in April. *I'm a detective,* she thought. *So okay, just a store detective and not a real one, but a detective, damn it, and what the hell am I doing here when some rat-fink shitepoke is out to get my father and me? This is worse than staying home. I gotta do something!* She started up the car and went back to Savage Point.

She drove past her house. She didn't want to listen to the blather of the maids. Greg was working with one of Doran's crews on the next block. He waved, but she didn't stop. No matter where one went in Savage Point at this time of year there was the ubiquitous lawn crew. And the security patrol car. After a while you scarcely noticed them, like the Con Edison people forever probing for leaks in their ancient gas pipes.

She wound up in front of Ralph Simmons's house on Dover Street and saw immediately that her timing was bad.

Ralph was putting a picnic basket in their VW Rabbit, and Lillian was closing the front door of the house. He was dressed in a form-fitting navy turtleneck that neatly accentuated the chubbiness of his figure. Not too bad for a retired man in his early sixties, she thought.

Lillian saw her first and bounded toward her crying, "It's Lisa, Ralph! How about that, here she is, in person!" She beamed at Lisa. "We were just talking about you, sweetheart. Honest, we called your house and got one of those strange women. I can never understand what they're saying."

She opened the door of Lisa's car. "Come on, come on, you're coming with us! Did you know that Ralph finally broke down and bought a boat? He lived here twenty years and never had a boat, and now he has one. It was such a bargain, only ten thousand dollars. Of course, we can't afford even that, but we said, What the devil, you only live once, right? And it's such a glorious day. Come on, come on." She hauled Lisa out of the car.

Ralph was there beside her, smiling and shaking his head at his wife's exuberance.

The boat, named the *Dry Martini,* was a sedate motor launch badly in need of scraping and painting, moored far from the dock in the middle of Little Neck Bay. Lisa, lost in her own pea-soup thoughts, helped unbutton and fold the tarp, watched while Ralph blew out the bilge and started the motor. She untied the line from the buoy, then Ralph told her to take the wheel.

He said, "It'll keep you busy and keep away the scary thoughts."

She grinned.

After putt-putting past the other moored boats, she opened the throttle and zoomed as fast as the old bucket could go toward the open water of Long Island Sound. She zigged and zagged to increase the sensation of motion and imagined she was racing against real speedboats for the championship of the world.

Ralph reached into the cabinet beside her and took out a bottle of pills. He took two, replaced the bottle, and disappeared below.

When he returned, she said, "What was that for?"

"The pills?" he said. "Just a precaution. After I bought the damn thing I discovered I was subject to seasickness. Isn't that a kick in the pants?"

"That's funny," she said. "My father has the same problem. After he bought the plane he found he's liable to get upchucky when the air is bumpy. So he takes air-sick pills just like you."

"Some travelers, your father and me," Ralph said. "Maybe it's God's way of saying, Keep your feet on the ground and don't be a wise guy."

Lisa asked if God really talks to a person that way.

"Well, now," he said vaguely. Then he said, "There's Co-op City rising like Camelot out of the waters of Avalon. Aren't they an abomination? Keep her heading toward City Island, I'm going down and get the helmsman for the next shift."

Lillian, dressed in a windbreaker, came back with him, saying, "Lunch is ready any time you want to eat." She had so far spent most of her time fussing around below, out of the wind and sun, yet her face was a blooming red. She was nervous about taking the wheel. "What if another boat comes?" she asked. Ralph told her not to worry, he and Lisa would be right there in the wheelhouse with her.

When Ralph and Lisa were settled facing each other, he said to Lisa, "Tell us about it."

So Lisa started talking. During her recitation Lillian had several crises—a log in the water, a seagull swooping at the windshield then perching there and staring at her, a freighter crossing her bow a half mile ahead—and each time Lisa's thoughts became confused. When she finished talking, Ralph asked questions until he felt he had the full picture.

"What do the police think of all this?" he asked.

"Yuk, how can there be so many dumb people on the police force?" she said. "Do they have to pass a dumbness test to get appointed? The chief dumdum says a ski mask is a ski mask and Mr. Raymond couldn't tell one from another in the dark. They think he made the whole story up to get himself off the hook."

"But it was an unusual ski mask?"

Lisa half grinned. "Wild," she said. "The old Cat Woman started to knit a wool sweater for Grampa, but her arthritis was acting up and she was afraid she wouldn't finish it, so for some nutty reason she turned it into a ski mask. It had orange cats all over it, except they didn't look like cats, just blobs."

"One of a kind," Ralph said. "How do the police explain it being out of place in the closet?"

"They say Pops didn't know what he was talking about," she said with scornful exasperation. "A man like him is never orderly, they say. A man without a wife, his closets are a mess."

"They have a point," Ralph said. "Who has the mask now?"

"They do."

"So they'll be examining it for strands of hair, whether the guy had dandruff and whether he was left-handed. They can find out a lot from a thing like that."

"Don't hold your breath," Lisa said.

Lillian said, "You gotta keep your hopes up, sweetie. The cops can't be as stupid as you make them out to be."

"Wanta bet?" Lisa said.

Ralph said, "About the claw, do the cops have that, too?"

"They collect things, that's what they're good at," Lisa replied.

"Did they find any fingerprints on the claw?"

"They couldn't find a kid's prints on a cookie jar."

"Did they check the placement of the prongs, you know, against the marks on your grandfather's throat?"

"Didn't match," Lisa said shortly. She took a deep breath. "The marks on Gramps were closer together. My father tried to tell them—that—" She swallowed hard. "My father tried to tell them that it makes a difference if—if the neck is stretched—"

"I get the point," Ralph said. "So as far as they're concerned, it's still the dog."

Lisa nodded, unable to speak.

Lillian spoke up. "Now *that* sounds dumb," she said.

They moored at City Island, had their picnic lunch in the open cockpit, strolled along the main street of the island, and marveled that the little seaport was actually a part of New York City.

On the return trip Ralph took Lisa to the rear of the boat and said, "When is your father going back to Albany?"

"Tomorrow."

"While he's up there, I don't think it would be wise for you to stay in the house alone. No big deal, just that you're invited to bunk down with us, at least for a few days. What do you say?"

Lisa stared at him steadily. "Then you think some killer is out to get the Honeywells?"

Ralph frowned. "I don't think one way or the other. But why take the chance when we have more rooms than we know what to do with?"

"But there might be?"

Ralph nodded. "It's possible. There's something weird going on, and until we find out what it is it's smart to go on the assumption that you may be in danger."

Lisa sat on his lap and kissed him. "Thank you, Uncle Ralph. I was beginning to think I was crazy."

Lillian called back from the wheelhouse in mock outrage, "Here! Here! I saw that!"

Ralph said, "Keep your eyes on the road, damn it."

Lisa returned to her chair. "It's a nice invitation," she said. "But I guess I'm going to Albany with Pops. He thinks I need protection, and I think he needs protection, and we both think we need a change of scene. So—"

He nodded. "It's probably a smart move. How good a pilot is your father?"

"Like he's driving a school bus," she said. "He's very careful—until he gets up past Poughkeepsie." She grinned. "Then he's like a kid in a demolition derby. It's fun."

Ralph frowned but didn't comment.

Lisa took the wheel for the last leg of the trip into Little Neck Bay. When she was parallel to the northern tip of Savage Point she slowed the boat. They were heading into the cluster of moored boats. Suddenly the glass windshield beside her shattered and showered her with shards. She cried, "Hey!"

The normal person would have remained frozen in place or have crouched down out of harm's way. Lisa was abnormal in this respect. A week ago she might well have cringed, but the sequence of shocks she had experienced had cracked her civilized veneer and uncovered a deep animal instinct: when threatened and cornered the animal instinctively lashes back at the attacker and, making contact, fights blindly to the death. A wild rage overwhelmed her. She swung the wheel to the left, pushed the throttle to full power, and headed directly toward the point on the Savage Point shore where her peripheral vision had caught the glint of sun on steel.

It was an area on Shore Road north of the Honeywell house where the foliage was thickest. Her eyes were fixed on the spot seeking movement that would give away the location of the sniper. She had no idea of what she would do when she came to the sea wall; somewhere in her head was the vague idea that she would force the bloody turd of a bushwhacker to show himself, then she would grapple with him and smash him to the ground.

Suddenly Ralph Simmons was beside her, shoving her roughly aside and spinning the wheel violently to the right, at the same time cutting off the motor. Sprawled on the deck, she heard the sound of the side of the boat scraping against a boulder. In the silence that ensued, she heard the heavy breathing of Ralph, a roaring in her own ears, and the lapping of water against the boat.

She opened her eyes—the startled face of Lillian was peering at her. It was at deck level and looked ridiculously like an oval red balloon with ash-blond hair on top. Lisa pushed herself to a sitting position, feeling the broken glass under her hands. She rested her head on her knees for a moment, then remembering the sniper, clambered to her feet.

Ralph was slumped against the wheel, breathing hard. She saw that the boat was rocking in the water only about ten feet from the great boulders at the base of the sea wall and about a hundred feet from the clump of foliage in which the sniper had been hiding.

He glanced at her and said, "What the hell did you think you were doing?"

The accusation in the question stung. Her sweet Uncle Ralph had never spoken to her so harshly before. "Going after the bastard who shot at us!" she shouted. "What do you think broke the window? It was a goddam bullet, that's what it was! He was right there! I saw him!"

Ralph flicked a glance in the direction she was pointing, then turned his gaze back to her. "What were you going to do?" he said more calmly. "Run over him with the boat? Plow through the boulders, climb a ten-foot sea wall, and pin him to the ground?"

"Well, like flush him out and get a look at him," she said, still resentful at Ralph's anger.

Lillian cried in bewilderment from below, "What's going on, you two? What are we doing over here, for crying out loud?"

Ralph made a face. "Lisa thought we wanted our *Dry Martini* on the rocks," he said. "I thought that wasn't such a good idea, that's all. Now if it's okay with you ladies, I'm taking over as captain and moving this magnificent craft away from danger. You will notice that we are once again drifting toward disaster and shipwreck."

He started the motor.

Lisa lunged down the stairs past Lillian, crying, "Wait, let me off! I'm going after the rat!"

Ralph swung the boat away from shore. "No, you're not, honey," he said. "Hang on to her, Lil."

As the two women wrestled clumsily, he said loudly, "He's probably no longer there, Lisa. You probably scared the pants off him. I know I'd be scared if you came at me with a rampaging heap like this. But if he's still there—honey, listen—if he's still there, he still has the gun. Remember? It's the thing he broke our window with. Are you going to tackle a man with a gun? That's not very bright, is it?" He shot a fleeting glance at the women.

"Now simmer down and let Lillian brush the glass out of your hair. You look like you have a star-spangled halo. Here's a joke. You remind me of the Statue of Liberty. Why do you remind me of the Statue of Liberty? Because you each have a hollow head."

He kept talking long after Lisa had ceased struggling and had plopped into one of the canvas chairs. Lillian was in another chair, gasping. "Boy, you fight dirty," Lillian said. "Where'd you learn that knee action? Lucky I wasn't a man. Whoo-ee."

Lisa apologized to her. She apologized to Ralph when he finally moored the boat. She was sincerely sorry for nearly crashing the boat on the rocks. She was sorry for putting them in danger by going with them when she knew someone was out to harm her. And deep within her the rage still burned, a killing rage.

But the strongest emotion she felt was fright, not of the hidden gunman—though there was that, too—no, for the first time in her life she had frightened herself. She had taken pride in her quick reflexes, imagining herself the Western lawperson who could outdraw any young punk who challenged her. But this time her reaction had been irrational. That was frightening. She had learned something unpleasant about herself. Her reactions couldn't be trusted.

Lieutenant Joseph Carbine of the 111th Precinct introduced himself. He looked like an aging movie star. A tall, rangy man in a light gray suit, hatless, he rested his rear end on the guard rail at the side of Shore Road, and looked down at the glassine envelope in his hand. The envelope contained a lone cartridge shell.

"Nothing unusual," he said. "It's a Springfield shell that can be used in a lot of different rifles. Who around here has a rifle?"

He directed the question at Ralph Simmons, who had protective arms around the shoulders of both Lillian and Lisa. Ralph said, "None that I know of. Shotguns,

I know a few shotguns, but no rifles. How about your friends, sweetie?" he said to Lisa.

She scowled and shook her head. She felt numb, withdrawn. She knew that Greg Muldavin had a rifle because he had showed it to her. Proudly. But the code of the rebellious teenager was still part of her, and one didn't rat on one's boyfriend.

Carbine was saying to Ralph, "We just don't know, sir. It could have been a stray shot, some damn fool shooting at a seagull and missing. That's a possibility. And it could have been someone with a rifle and a grudge. Who knew you'd be out in the boat today?"

Ralph gestured helplessly toward the open bay. "There must have been forty or fifty people who saw us go. Could have been anyone."

"Someone who had a grudge against you?"

Ralph shook his head. "Not that I know of."

Lisa had to smile. She knew that Ralph Simmons didn't have an enemy in the world; he spent much of his time, too much of his time, trying to make people like him. Some people looked down on him for it.

Ralph said, "I think you should listen to Lisa Honeywell's story."

The lieutenant smiled faintly at Lisa. "I know her story," he said. "Do you think this is part of the plot, Lisa?"

She didn't like his use of her first name. He was the "chief dumdum," and he was treating her like a child. "No," she said. "Different M.O., Joe."

Carbine's smile broadened, then vanished. "You mean this was the first time a gun was used."

"You got it, Joe. Whoever's after us is playing games. But you don't believe that, do you?"

Carbine lowered his eyes. "I'm sorry I offended you, Miss Honeywell," he said. "Look, I won't call you by your first name if you don't call me by mine. Okay?"

Lisa shrugged, annoyed with herself. She was acting like a resentful child.

"As for what I believe," Carbine went on, "I don't know. You and your father have been going through a hard time. But there *are* such things as coincidences. They don't necessarily form a pattern. And if the shooting today is not part of the pattern—I mean, if the person with the rifle was not shooting at a specific individual named Lisa Honeywell but at a faceless person at the controls of a moving boat in the middle of the bay, then I'm afraid this was the debut of a random sniper."

He grimaced. "There seems to be an epidemic of them going around. There's that murderous moron out on the expressway, and there are others across the country. They pick on cars, passenger trains, and now boats. I hope I'm wrong, but it looks like that's what we have here—a madman with a rifle and an urge to wing people on the move."

Ralph Simmons had a stern look on his face. "What you're saying is that Lisa and her father are not in danger, that it's all a coincidence."

Carbine sighed and stood up. "What I'm saying is that there are a lot of explanations including, *including* a plot against the Honeywells. And this time the killer has given us something to go on."

"The gun?"

Carbine nodded. "And the odds are the sniper is a resident. A stranger would be noticed even if he hid the rifle in a package or something. All we have to do is find the rifle."

Ralph glanced at the houses on the other side of Shore Road and shook his head skeptically.

Lillian demanded to know, "What about Lisa?"

"We've been keeping an eye on her, ma'am," Carbine said. He walked off to join the policemen who were just finishing their search of the thicket. They seemed to have come away empty-handed.

Lisa walked with the Simmonses back along Shore Road toward the dock, where Ralph had parked his car. One of Jack Doran's garden crews was working on the Honeywell grounds. Greg Muldavin turned off his mower and loped across the lawn to intercept them. He held Lisa at arm's length and peered down into her eyes.

"Are you okay?" he asked.

"Why shouldn't I be?" she said. "I had a nice afternoon on the water. What did you do?"

"What do you mean, what did I do? I was working! I saw you nearly plow into the wall. What happened?"

Ralph and Lillian walked on to say a few words to Doran, who had apparently stopped by to check on his crew.

Lisa said, "Didn't you get time off for lunch?"

"Sure, but—"

She drifted away from him. "I have to get my car. I'll see you tonight."

Greg stood with slumped shoulders and watched her rejoin the Simmonses.

Paul Doran rolled by in the security patrol car and greeted Lisa with a toot on the horn.

Jack Doran said, "And here's the lovely Miss Lisa." He hugged her to convey sympathy. "I can't imagine anyone wanting to shoot at you, sweetheart. It must have been a crazy person for sure."

She extracted herself from his embrace and said that he was probably right. "A crazy for sure."

Doran said, "You take care of yourself, y'hear?"

Lisa said she would.

At the dock she noticed Meg Webster sitting on a bench alone, holding a paperback book as if she were reading it. She was dressed in a light pink bathing suit, which accentuated her rotundity. Lisa idly made a mental note to suggest a darker color. Her brother Bruce was with his fellow dock rats at the shore end of the pier seemingly engrossed in their snickering inanities. He was dressed only in tan shorts, and Lisa noticed that his midriff was thickening. She had the impression that his attention was on her and he was trying to hide it.

Getting into his little car, Ralph Simmons said, "Thus ends a delightful day of punting on the sound."

Lillian said, "Really, Ralph."

Lisa didn't say anything. In her mind she saw the sniper skulking in the sparse cover of foliage atop the sea wall and pointing the rifle at the wheelhouse of the *Dry Martini*. The sniper looked directly at her, but she couldn't conjure a face to go with the figure. Blank.

Seven

THEY WERE IN Greg's room. His father was at a business convention in White Sulphur Springs, and his mother had gone with him. Greg and Lisa had the house to themselves. Lisa lay on the bed gazing at the Merchant Marine Academy pennant on the opposite wall. The posters that covered the rest of the wall told the story of Greg Muldavin—parachutists plummeting, fighter planes zooming, skiers soaring, Bruce Lee kicking, divers plunging, a tiger charging, grizzly bear rearing, and a pink-skin pride of *Playboy* centerfolds—dreams of wild adventure and feverish sex, the teenager father to the twenty-one-year-old boy.

Ordinarily she liked looking at his strong, lean body, but tonight other thoughts intruded.

He came to her, and she said, "What kind of bullets do you use in your rifle?"

He froze in the act of reaching for her. "How's that again?" he asked.

She said, "I was just wondering." She gave him a patently insincere smile. Ever since the shooting on the bay, the sense of being a stationary target for a stalking killer had become intolerable, and the need to strike back was overwhelming. But there was nothing to strike back *at*. The detective in her was impelled to investigate, but she didn't know where to begin. Frustration forced the question out of her. Vaguely she realized that her timing was atrocious and that she had deflated Greg's only-too-vulnerable image of himself as the Great Lover.

He grabbed the pillow from beneath her head and flung it violently across the room. The lack of any smashing noise infuriated him further. He kicked the bed and spun it halfway around. Finally he snatched up his alarm clock and hurled it at his desk. The crash was satisfying. "What kind of a damn question was that?" he said.

He slumped into a chair across the room.

She went to him and started the cajoling process. She told him he was the greatest bed partner in all of Savage Point. He asked her how she knew that. She said, Because nobody could be better. She tried to slide into his lap and ended on the floor. She exaggerated her injury, and he said he was sorry. She apologized for her dumb question, saying that the devil made her do it. She wound up in his lap and shortly thereafter in bed.

Later, propped against the headboard, she said, "Promise you won't take this wrong."

He glanced at her sideways. "You're going to ask the same question, aren't you?"

"Yes, yes I am!" she shouted. "And you're going to answer, damn it, unless you're the one who took a potshot at me."

He put a hand on her thigh. "You know I'd never do that, sweetie," he said softly.

"Okay, okay, I'm not accusing or anything, I just want to know. What kind of rifle do you have?"

He stirred. "I'll get it."

She said, "Never mind. Just tell me."

He said, "It's a Winchester. I'll get it." He went to his closet and brought back the gleaming rifle. He thrust it at her, and she had to take it to keep the cold metal from touching her bare skin. Though the strong smell of oil reminded her reassuringly of her Firebird's motor, she shuddered.

"Is it loaded?"

"No, silly, nobody keeps a loaded gun lying around." He went to his bureau, rummaged in the bottom drawer, and came back to her. "This is a box of cartridges. They fit in the magazine here, three in a magazine—"

"Let me see." She took one of the bullets and peered at it. "I can't make it out," she said. "Are these Springfield bullets?"

"No, sweetie, they're Winchesters."

"Would a Springfield fit?"

He sighed. "It might, I don't know. There are all kinds and sizes. What you have there is a Winchester cartridge. A Winchester for a Winchester."

"You're mad, aren't you?"

"No. How could I be mad at you?"

"I can't help it if you're mad, I gotta find out," she said. "Who else on the Point has a rifle?"

He looked at her blankly. "Maybe it sounds funny, but I don't know. All my old friends are away at college. I know two of them that have rifles, but they're not here. I've gabbed with some of the guys on the crew, about my Winnie, but as far as I know, none of them have rifles. Gee, honey, I'll ask around."

When she was leaving for home, she said, "The police are going to be here asking questions. Don't get mad at them, okay?"

It was Marcus Honeywell who was mad, in both senses of the word. He was in one of his animal-in-a-zoo moods, pacing aimlessly, making guttural sounds. At the end of his workday, during which he had become increasingly restive, his partner Eddie Epstein had taken him home for a therapeutic drinking session. But poor Eddie had tried to keep up with him, and Marcus had had to put him to bed, then had come home to find Lisa's note that she had gone out with Greg Muldavin.

Now it was Lisa's turn to put her father to bed. He was being excessively emotional. She insisted that he drink a glass of milk on the theory that it was a sobering and soothing potion. She guided him up the stairs. He told her he didn't need any help. In his bedroom she sat him on the side of his bed, and he immediately bounced to his feet.

"I feel I'm in a blindfolded wrestling match," he wailed. "I'm being walloped from all sides, but all I can grab hold of is air."

"I know what you mean," she said.

He hugged her. "At least I'm getting you out of here. You'll be safe in Albany. Are you all packed?"

"Sure, Pops."

"Take along a nice dress, will you do that for me? You look so beautiful when you're dressed up the way a lady should be. I want to show you off up there, I'll be so proud. 'Who's that gorgeous creature with Honeywell?' they'll ask. 'She must be a movie star.' That's what you are, Lisa. My movie star."

She said, "I'll take a dress, Pops."

"Be ready at the crack of dawn," he said.

He slept restlessly. She could hear his movements on the mattress from the next room. In her own bed she stared at the ceiling for a long time, thinking of her handsome, loving father who was going to take her two hundred miles away from Savage Point to make sure that she would be safe. But at the same time he was taking *himself* away, and this was causing him anguish. In her short lifetime she had learned that men—boys really—had a ridiculous code of behavior. The old adage, *He who fights and runs away will live to fight another day,* was not for them. A man who did that would show himself to be a coward or at least a wimp, no matter how he tries to kid himself. It was unspoken, perhaps even unformulated, in her father's mind, but she knew he felt it because she sensed the same nonsensical motive in her own reactions to danger.

He loved her, she knew that. She was his "movie star." She was "gorgeous." Maybe that was one of the things that blocked close communication between her and her father. Her face. She tried to picture her face and couldn't. It was as blank as that of the sniper. If she saw herself walking along the street, would she recognize herself? A hundred million other people had features just like hers, and only the animation in her eyes distinguished Lisa from all the others. But suppose the eyes were dead. What would she look like in a coffin? A mannequin, a dummy. Nothing.

After a while she was asleep. In the middle of the night she heard cautious footsteps in the hall. "Are you all right, Pops?" she called. She heard what sounded like a reassuring grunt and went back to sleep.

Marcus Honeywell was an entirely different person in the morning. Tooling along the Cross Island Parkway in his Mark VII, he was bubbling with high spirits as if they were starting a carefree vacation. In fact, he spoke of running off to the Catskills on the weekend, just the two of them, starting at the game farm in Palenville, then up the Rip Van Winkle Trail to a really fun place he knew. Swinging under the Whitestone Bridge overpass, he sang, "We're off to see the gov'nor, the wonderful gov'nor of ours."

"Oz," she said. To her the good thing about his performance was that he wasn't doing it simply to cheer her up, he was doing it because he felt exhilarated to be away from Savage Point and heading toward something he really enjoyed—flying his lovely flying machine.

The day was sparklingly clear, one of those rare days when you felt you could see forever. She let herself be caught up in his mood, watched the little planes buzzing around Flushing Airport like bees around a hive and the lumbering monsters sliding down an invisible chute to LaGuardia across Flushing Bay. She liked the little ones better because they looked like they were playing. That was the ticket: get your father away from death and danger, have fun with him in the playgrounds of Albany. She grinned to herself at the idea of having fun in the state legislature. Maybe she could shoot some spitballs from the gallery at the self-important political upstarts below.

At Flushing Airport Marcus did all the necessary things while she trailed behind. He parked the car in his regular spot, let Lisa carry his attaché case while he toted her luggage to the gleaming electric blue plane. He conversed with some of the employees, and from their attitude she could tell they liked him.

Finally they were buckled in their seats, he in the pilot's seat and she alongside him. The jet engine whined, then roared into life. The sound must have reminded him, because he said, "Oops, almost forgot. Hand me the attaché case, honey." He opened it in his lap, took out a small thermos and a bottle of pills.

"My antibarf fix," he said, taking two pills and washing them down with water from the thermos.

She teased him by claiming the pills were acid and he was washing them down with vodka. He laughed, crossed his eyes, and said, "Whee!"

They taxied to the runway preparatory to taking off into the northwest wind. The route would take them over the houses of College Point to the East River, then a turn to the east to take them away from the LaGuardia landing pattern.

Marcus grunted and put a hand on his stomach.

"What's the matter?" she asked.

He relaxed. "Nothing, honey, just a leftover popover popping over in there, or something."

The voice in the earphone said, "You're cleared, Honeywell. Remember the password—cut taxes."

"Got it, George," Marcus said, smiling.

"Luck," the voice said.

Marcus gunned the jets causing the whole plane to vibrate. Then he unleashed them, and the plane roared down the runway and at the last moment zoomed into the air. This was the part that Lisa loved best, the thrusting escape from gravity. She laughed like the child she still was.

A hundred feet up . . . two hundred feet up . . . the houses below them, the blue-gray East River ahead, and off to the right the two magnificent bridges that tied the borough of Queens to the Bronx. She and her father were gods of the sky peering down at the land-locked insect colony that was the rest of the human race.

Suddenly her father made a rasping noise and his body became rigid; the contracting muscles of his arms pulled the plane into a precipitous climb, then just as suddenly the body slumped forward, pushing the plane into a steep dive.

Lisa's first thought was that her father was playing an uncharacteristically foolhardy game, right within sight of the air controllers! She screamed, "Pops!" They were plunging at two hundred miles an hour down into the houses of College Point.

Her reactions were just as sudden. Her father was apparently unconscious, his hundred-and-eighty-pound body a dead weight on the controls locking the plane in its deadly plunge. Time was measured not in seconds but in milliseconds. Without conscious thought, she released her seat belt, grabbed her father by both shoulders and yanked him back, then chopped down with her forearm breaking his grip on the wheel. She couldn't remove him from the pilot's seat, however, and didn't have time to find the release button on his seat belt.

A lone high-rise apartment building seemed to reach out of the carpet of foliage and private houses, and draw the plane to it. On its roof was a large dish antenna. To Lisa's frantic gaze it was a bull's-eye and she was speeding straight into its center. The perimeter of the dish was expanding outward to receive her, and she fancied that it would close around her and digest her like one of the strange plants she had seen on television.

Reaching sideways over her father, she yanked the control wheel backward; the plane screeched in protest as it bottomed out, shuddered momentarily, almost halted, then started for the sky at an impossible eighty-degree climb. The jets coughed, and she sensed they were about to stall. She eased up on the wheel, and the plane straightened into a less precipitous climb.

A shrill voice came on the radio. "Flushing, what the hell's going on over there?"

George's voice came quickly: "Plane acting erratically. Will try to call it back in."

Lisa heard the voices because the headset had come off her father's head. Still clutching the wheel with one hand, she placed the receiver to her ear with the other.

George: "Honeywell, level off, you're too high! Level off!"

Lisa pushed the wheel forward, and the plane went into a slight decline.

George: "What in hell do you think you're doing?"

Lisa: "My father's sick. This is Lisa."

George (loudly): "I can hardly hear you. Speak into the mike!"

Lisa: "I can't. I'm holding the wheel with one hand and the ear thing with the other. What should I do?"

George: "What's the matter with Honeywell?"

Lisa: "He's unconscious. What should I do, damn it?"

George: "Can you fly?"

Lisa: "No."

George: "Wonderful . . .! Okay, turn the wheel to the right and head back here. I'll tell you what to do when you get close. It's just like driving a car, Lisa. You drive, don't you?"

She turned the wheel to the right. The altimeter showed five hundred feet. She was bent awkwardly sideways over her father's body, barely able to see over the instrument panel with all its confusing gauges and gadgets. She could see enough to know she had just flown over the Whitestone Bridge and was over the Whitestone section of Queens.

Lisa: "Yeah, I drive, George. There's only one trouble. In a car you don't have to worry about landing gear."

George: "Don't worry about landing yet, honey. I'll tell you how to work it when it's time."

Lisa: "Listen to me, man. The landing gear got smashed on an antenna. I don't think it'll work."

George (softly): "Shit." (More loudly): "Keep coming the way you are. It'll take you right over the field here, and we'll get a look at it. You're doing great, honey. Hang in there."

During the following period of silence, she nudged her father with her hip. "Pops!" she yelled. "Come on, Pops!"

The radio crackled.

George: "It's smashed all right. We'll have to bring you down in a pancake landing. Nothing to worry about, honey. It'll be just like falling into a feather bed."

Lisa: "Bull cookies, George! I'd be a pancake all right, a burned pancake. Why don't I just stay up here till my father wakes up? He'll know what to do."

The plane was back over the East River, about a hundred feet above it, still in the same downward spiral.

George: "I hate to suggest this, honey, but I want you to put down the earphone and try to feel for your father's pulse. The side of the neck is a good place. Try that, will you, sweetie?"

That damned George, she knew how to take a pulse! This was a serious waste of time. Of course, her father had a pulse, everybody had a pulse. She knew the general location of the carotid artery, and she stretched to touch her father's neck, momentarily unable to see out of the windscreen.

Her fingers found no pulse. Damn, she was doing it wrong! How could she feel a pulse when the whole plane was vibrating. She straightened—

The span of the Whitestone Bridge was dead ahead of her. In a millisecond she had to make a choice—to go over the span or under. Since the plane was already descending and a change of direction upward might not clear the suspension cables of the bridge in time, she shoved the wheel forward and closed her eyes.

George's voice was coming at her from somewhere. He was shouting. She forced her eyes open. What a dumb little-girl thing to do! Her peripheral vision saw a confused seagull get sucked into the left jet, killing the engine. The plane shuddered, veered sharply left and downward straight toward the choppy water. She screamed.

Even as she screamed, a voice within her was saying, it's just like a blowout, you stupid nerd; if the left tire goes, you steer right, remember that time on the expressway—

She turned the wheel hard right and pulled backward. The tip of the left wing nicked the surface of the water . . . and came out. Awkwardly using both hands, she righted the level of the plane, noting that she had to readjust the direction every few seconds to keep it flying.

The headset had fallen somewhere, and she didn't have hands enough to grope for it.

She shouted: "George, is water softer than land?"

She heard George's voice but couldn't make out what he was saying. From the little she knew about radar she realized that she must have dropped out of the radar's scope.

She shouted: "We're fifteen feet over the river heading toward the other bridge. Oops, just missed the mast of a freighter." She struggled to bank the plane away from the ship. "Sorry, feller," she muttered to a wide-eyed crewman.

One word came through George's muffled chatter. *Throttle.* The Throgs Neck Bridge loomed ahead of her. Her awkward position was beginning to pain her, and her head was starting to swim giddily. Her whole attention had to be focused on what lay ahead.

"Hey, Pops, where the hell's the throttle?" she said. She permitted herself swift glances at the instrument panel. None of it made sense. Was the throttle on the floor like in a car, or was it one of these damn knobs and levers on the crazy dash?

The plane careened erratically under the Throgs Neck Bridge, about ten feet above the water. She knew where she was. "Just a little old right turn into Little Neck Bay and we're home, Pops," she said through clenched teeth.

It took all her strength to make the turn around Fort Totten and into the cove, now duplicating yesterday's route of the *Dry Martini,* only through the air instead of water. Savage Point lay ahead to the left. Now what? "Pops," she cried. "What do I do?" She managed to avoid the masts of the anchored pleasure boats. The plane was now sliding toward the marsh at the head of the bay.

"This is it, Pops," she said. "End of the line."

She eased the plane downward, still going much too fast to land anywhere except on a long runway. An abrupt stop would mean a crash and smashed bodies. Instinct told her what to do. Just as the bottom of the plane was touching the marsh reeds, she pulled back a little on the controls with one hand while she slammed all the instruments on the panel with the other, hoping that one of them would cut off the engine and bring the plane to a halt.

The last thing she did was ease the wheel forward for the landing in the marsh. Her head hit the instrument panel, and all systems stopped.

The sun exploded, and died in blackness.

Eight

HER BRAIN was short-circuited. It crackled with static, gave her flashes of sight, then blackouts. She was on top of her father. Blackout. No, her father was on top of her, oh God, she couldn't breathe. Blackout. She stirred, she was lying in water! But the weight, the awful weight was gone, she took a breath, and blacked out. She was being carried, she could see the electric-blue plane. Upside down. Nose down, leaning against the railroad embankment. Train stopped, people staring. Whirling blades overhead. Sound overwhelming. She was drowning in sound . . .

"Where am I?"
"Booth Memorial."
"Never heard of it."

"I told Marc not to buy that plane. I told him not to buy it, didn't I, Eddie? And now look what he's done . . .! You're awake, darling. How do you feel? Is your mouth dry? Here, let me hold the water for you."

Lisa said something.

Her mother said, "What was that, sweetheart?"

"Where's Pops?"

"Well now, don't you worry about your father. We have to get you well and strong. No, don't turn away . . ."

The next time she woke up, she tried to return to unconsciousness and couldn't. Her headache grew in intensity, but what she fiercely wanted to escape from was a mental agony, a grief so unbearable that she tried with all her might to hold it at bay.

She opened her eyes and had to squint because of the glaring whiteness. She was in a hospital, that was obvious. Her hand groped for something to hug, something that would reassure her that she was safe from the bad things that were out there. But the little lamb of her childhood wasn't there, she had thrown it on the floor of her closet years ago along with other toys of her infancy. She flicked her head sideways in self-disapproval. She was a grown-up now, damn it, and didn't need silly kid things anymore.

She peered at the man sitting beside her bed, a man with a craggy face and tightly curled red hair. His eyes were open, gazing not at her, however, but at something inside himself that gave his stubbled face a look of deep sadness.

"Uncle Eddie?"

He focused on her. "Hey, Lisa my love, welcome back to the land of the living." His face was beaming. "You were doing a Rip Van Winkle number on us, kid.

Welcome back, damn it!" And her father's hard-boiled law partner reached out and clasped her hand.

She had trouble getting her words out. "He's dead, isn't he?"

The hand tightened on hers. "Well now, I think I'd better let the police lieutenant tell you about—" Epstein stopped his flow of words. Then he nodded somberly. "Yes, Marcus is dead. We've all suffered a great loss—"

Tears filled her eyes. "I blew it, Uncle Eddie," she said. "I thought I could bring that flying shitepoke down nice and easy in the mud flat, and I *crashed* the blue bastard! What do they call someone who kills her father? I didn't do it on purpose, but I should have been able to—"

"Now wait a minute, honey," Epstein cut in. "The *crash* didn't kill Marcus! You did a hell of a job getting that plane down, you're a bloody heroine, for God's sake, don't go thinking things like that about yourself . . .! Wait, let me get the lieutenant, he's right out in the hall, he'll tell you what killed your father. Just hold on a minute!"

He went to the door and returned with the police lieutenant, the one who had spoken to her on Shore Road, what was his name—like a gun. Carbine. He looked like he needed a shave, too.

He stood tall beside the bed and looked down at her. "It's good to see you awake," he said.

She said, slurring her words, "Hello, Joe, whaddiya know?"

He gave a tight smile. "And your same old feisty self."

"What killed my father?"

"You're a very direct person, aren't you? So I'll be direct. You'll have to be told sooner or later . . . Your father died of cyanide poisoning. We recovered his attaché case, so we know how it was administered."

"The water," she said.

"No, the pills. Every pill in the bottle was doctored. What we want you to do is fill in the gaps."

Epstein said, "I thought they could do that only with capsules."

"These were pills, sir. It can be done. Now tell me what happened, Lisa. I like calling you Lisa, is that okay?"

"No problem, Joe."

The pain in her head receded while she related the events of the morning.

Carbine said, "You took your father's attaché case and put it in the plane."

"Yes."

"Could anyone at the airport have gotten to it from the time you arrived there to the time you took off?"

"No, I got in the plane at the same time and was sitting right there with it."

"So it had to have been done before you left the house."

"I don't see how. There was only my father and me."

"Where did he keep the attaché case when he was home?"

"In his study."

"Where is that?"

"On the second floor, to the right when you go up."

"As far as you know, did he open it at any time while he was home?"

Lisa shook her head, causing the pain to inch back. "It was just something he carried back and forth from Albany and on trips. It was his emergency kit if he got stuck somewhere. Well, you saw what was in there."

Carbine said, "Clean shirt, underwear, socks, razor, toothbrush, comb, aspirin, a book of crossword puzzles, the thermos—he wouldn't leave the same water in there, would he? He must have filled it with fresh water each time."

"I guess so," Lisa said. "But I didn't actually see him."

"So he must have opened it at least once, and probably yesterday morning."

"Yesterday!" Lisa cried. "What do you mean, yesterday?"

Carbine glanced at Epstein, then back to Lisa. "I assumed you knew," he said. "You've been out cold for twenty-four hours. This is Tuesday."

Lisa said, "Shit." Her mind went blank for a moment.

Carbine said, "Aside from you and your father, who else was in your house in the last five days?"

"Well, the maids—"

"We've talked to them. Who else?"

"Nobody . . . only the killer."

Carbine looked puzzled, then he said, "The fire in the kitchen?"

"That . . . and other things."

"There was something about a ski mask."

"You got it, Joe."

"Looks like he had the run of the house. How could that be? Don't you lock your doors at night?"

She pulled her eyes away from his. "Sometimes," she said.

"Great."

"My father was absentminded."

"You, too, it seems."

"I guess so."

"So you had a sign outside saying 'Welcome to Burglars'."

"There are no burglars in Savage Point! People trust each other!"

"That's dumb, Lisa. We have figures at the precinct that say otherwise."

"So you got figures." she said sullenly.

Carbine shook his head as if to clear it. "Do you have any thoughts on who this person might be?"

Lisa shook her head miserably. "I think I need an aspirin," she said.

The police lieutenant left. Eddie Epstein summoned the nurse, who gave Lisa two extra-strength Tylenol. The nurse said, "Lucky you have a hard head, honey. You have a beaut of a concussion."

"Is that all I have?"

"What do you want? A broken leg, too? Be happy with a concussion, dearie."

Lisa started to drift off to sleep. Eddie Epstein was still there. She said, "Uncle Eddie, about my father—"

He took her hand. "Let me handle all that," he said. "Everything's under control."

She squeezed his hand. "I—I think he'd like a sporty casket. Something in electric blue maybe."

"I don't think they have that color. Don't worry, I'll pick a good one."

"My mother was here."

"Yes, yesterday. In her own way, she loves you."

"Yeah, loves me to death. What makes her the way she is?"

"I don't think I know the answer to that one."

"About money."

"I'm executor of the will. You're a rich young lady."

"Great."

She drifted off.

The young resident was a card. "We CAT-scanned your brain, Lisa," he said.

"Yeah?"

"We didn't find anything."

Lisa turned away. "That's what my mother always said."

Her mother was back.

"When you're all better, sweetheart, you'll come live with me. Won't that be fun?"

"No."

"You're not yourself, Lisa. We'll talk about it later."

Lisa pictured herself living in her mother's East Side apartment, enclosed, gasping for air. She said, "It's nice of you to want me, Mom, and I love you for it, I really do, but I belong in Savage Point. I'd die in Manhattan."

Her mother laughed lightly. "A minor is not mature enough to know what's best for her," she said. "It's settled, so let's not talk about it anymore now. Let's talk about pleasant things."

"You see?" Lisa said. "Already you're calling me a child and making decisions for me. Mother, I'm not your baby anymore, I'm a detective, a grown-up detective, and I'm going to find out—"

"There you go," her mother retorted. "The same old adolescent dreams. Why your father let you become a store detective I'll never know. It's not—it's not *becoming* for someone in your station in life. It's—it's—"

Lisa said with great dignity, "I'm going to sleep now, Mother. If you have anything further to say, talk to my lawyer!"

She turned over and faced away from her mother. After a moment she heard her mother say, "That proves it. Empty-headed, that's what you are."

Lisa grinned to herself.

The next day she was permitted to have visitors.

Her boyfriend Greg came and sat on the side of the bed. "Hello, Tiger," he said. "I didn't know you could fly a plane."

That made her laugh. "Not very good at landing, though."

They stayed with banter for a few minutes to avoid the more serious actualities. Then he said, "You were right. The police came to check on my guns."

"Guns? What do you mean, guns? The only one you showed me—"

"That's right. We were talking about rifles. That was the only *rifle* I have. But my father gave me a shotgun when I was sixteen, and I still have that. Then there are the handguns—"

"Damn it, Greg, you sound like a one-man army!"

"Can I help it if I like guns?"

As he got ready to leave, he shoved something to her under the blanket. "Something to have," he said. "Just in case."

She looked at it. It was the scuba knife in its leather case.

She shoved it back to him.

"Honestly, Greg, sometimes I think you're crazy."

After he left, she wondered if she shouldn't have kept the knife. There was a policeman outside the door to her room. But what good would he be if the killer sneaked in through the window while she was asleep? On the other hand, what good would the knife be if she was asleep? Well, no sense worrying about it, since she didn't have the knife anyway.

Ralph and Lillian Simmons, after first checking her mood, came on like stand-up comics. Since his retirement he had few sources of new jokes, but Lisa loved hearing his corny old ones. She thought of them as Golden Oldies.

Then Ralph turned serious and asked Lisa about her fatal plane trip. "After all, we've been sitting in that damned waiting room for forty-eight hours. I think we're entitled." So Lisa told them of her experiences, and found she could talk about them without getting the shakes. She also related the visit from her mother.

Ralph said, "Your mother's right in one respect. You can't go back to that house alone. Not right now anyway. Listen, honey child, there are just the two of us, and we have five bedrooms, clean sheets, and a view of our backyard, American plan, color TV, miniature golf course next door. Don't say yes or no, just think about it. You're invited to bunk with us. We have a killer cat guarding the premises, and the floors squeak so no one can sneak up on you. Oh, yes, and a gourmet cook with an eclectic cuisine. Hot dogs one day, and hamburgers the next. Macaroni and cheese is the specialty of the house. Tuna fish costs extra."

Lisa was laughing as he went on to cite other advantages of the house, such as hot and cold running water, indoor plumbing, access to the historic Honeywell mansion on Shore Road by appointment, free cruises on the *Dry Martini,* happy hour between five and six . . .

The next morning she was permitted to attend her father's funeral at the Savage Point church—in a wheelchair. "Just to be on the safe side," the doctor had said. "Concussions can be tricky things." The Savage Point Volunteer Ambulance Corps picked her up at the hospital in Flushing and brought her to the church. She was surprised to see that the driver was Jack Doran and the attendant was Eunice Webster. They both treated her like a celebrity, and even discounting the flattery and false jollity, Lisa felt closer to home because they were neighbors.

Doran, for once not wearing his usual Navy blazer, tugged at his pale-blue corps jacket and called himself her "caddy" for the day; he spoke of the steps to the church as a "chip shot" and carried the joke to tiresome extremes. Mrs. Webster covered her embarrassment at her husband's pending petition to take the family trust away from Marcus Honeywell by being extra solicitous of Lisa's comfort. Lisa thought it ironic that the killer had insured the success of Webster's campaign against her father.

Lisa endured the ordeal of the funeral in a dreamlike state. The modest church was crowded inside and out. She recognized some of the mourners as politicians, but she was somehow comforted to see that most of the people were friends and neighbors who had nothing to gain by her father's death. Some had tears in their eyes, and her own eyes welled.

The casket was dark and gleaming. Oh well, it was the best that Uncle Eddie could do. Casket makers had no imagination. Nobody is set adrift to Avalon anymore.

The minister spoke like a cornball Shakespearean actor, the organist rumbled, the choir sang, and Lisa, not hearing, gave way to bitterness. *I'm sorry I gave you a hard time, Pops. Look, I'm wearing a dress. Three cheers. I'm sorry I was snotty to you, Pops. The worst part is I never said I loved you. Always thinking about myself. Empty-headed. Mom was right. How could you put up with an empty-headed snot like me? Listen, I'm saying it. I love you. I love you . . . too late . . .*

She slumped in the pew and wept.

Afterward, people crowded around her while Doran helped her into the wheelchair. She didn't need help, damn it, but she let him do it because that was what he was supposed to do. Flashbulbs blinded her. Insensitive people crowded around her thinking they were being sensitive, her mother and the minister among them. She knew that Ralph and Lillian were there and old Tom Shakespeare, but they stayed their distance.

Meg Webster whispered something in her ear. It sounded like, "There's something I have to tell you," that was all. And her mother said, "No, you don't." Lisa didn't want to hear it anyway.

When they got outside, she saw that it was raining. Doran said, "Sorry, little girl, no cemetery. It's back to the hospital for you."

Lisa didn't object. She had to get well, to be strong enough to track down the killer.

Nine

Two days later Eddie Epstein reluctantly drove Lisa home. He wanted her to stay at his house for a few days, but she said, "Sorry, Uncle Eddie, you live out in left field, and nobody'd know where I was."

"That's the general idea," he said.

She said, "Come on, I'll be okay." She smiled sweetly. "Besides, there'll be a cop outside. Carbine promised."

Shore Road was a one-way street going south, and Epstein had to drive almost to the point and come back on Shore Road to get to Lisa's house. They passed the clump where the sniper had hidden. She spit at it.

Epstein pulled into her driveway and went into the house with her. "You're sure now?" he said.

She hugged him and said she was sure.

When he left, she went back outside with him. A police car had driven onto the driveway behind his car. "You see?" she said.

Then she was alone in the house. Outside, the sun was hot, but the house was cold. She hugged herself, feeling dizzy. The doctor had told her to expect occasional dizzy spells and to baby herself for a few weeks and not to play football.

"Nuts," she muttered, and went upstairs and took a long hot shower. Since she was alone in the house, there was no need to be modest. She roamed naked through the second-floor rooms, enjoying the sense of freedom. She studied herself in the mirror on her closet door. She wiggled her hips. "Too damn bony," she announced. "But not bad."

She had already put on her jeans when she tugged them off and donned a skirt and blouse. She had to live up to her father's image of her. She peered at herself in the mirror, shrugged, and said, "Could be worse."

Now for the task at hand: track down the killer.

Go step by step.

What was the first step?

She couldn't think of a first step. She suddenly felt terribly lonely.

Meg Webster wanted to tell her something. Probably nothing important, but since Lisa had nothing else to do at the moment . . . She went into her father's den and dialed Meg's number.

Eunice the mother answered.

"Oh, Lisa dear, you're home," she said. "I'm sorry, but you missed Meg by twenty-four hours. She left for the mountains yesterday."

"The mountains?"

"The Adirondacks, dear. Our place up there. Meg always loved her summers up there. After all, we got the place for the children. Malcolm is not the outdoors type, and Bruce loves the boat here more than roughing it on the lake, but Meg has turned into a regular Smoky the Bear." Mrs. Webster's laugh sounded idiotic.

Lisa was again feeling chilled. She knew that Meg hated the place in the mountains. "She wanted to tell me something," Lisa said. "Did she leave a message?"

"No-o. Maybe she just wanted to tell you she was going away. Very likely that's what it was. She'll be going directly from there to school in September, so heaven knows when you'll be able to see her again. But that's life, isn't it?"

When Lisa hung up, she wandered downstairs to the center hall. She saw something she hadn't noticed before—the grimy, threadbare toy from her childhood, the little white lamb she had cuddled in her bed until only a few years ago. It was perched on the hall table. The last time she had seen it, it was on the floor of her closet.

First, she got dizzy. Then she found she was sitting on the floor of the hall with the lamb in her arms. She stopped humming when she recognized the tune. "Lisa Had a Little Lamb." Her home was suddenly alien to her; familiar objects were somehow menacing. The damn concussion had scrambled her brains, she thought.

She jumped to her feet. *No, damn it, someone was playing games, had been from the beginning, the final move of which in each case was murder.* And it finally dawned on her that her powers of detection were pitifully inadequate in her quixotic quest for the killer, a quest that could only lead to her own death at a time and place chosen by the killer. She couldn't do it alone. She needed help . . .

The phone rang. She picked it up in the kitchen.

The voice said, "Eddie Epstein told us to keep an eye on you—"

Lisa blurted, "I'm coming over, Uncle Ralph. I—I need you." She had never said that to anyone in her life.

One of Ralph Simmons's idiosyncracies was a dislike for air conditioning, partially because he was a cigarette smoker and the stale smoke seemed to accumulate in the air-conditioned area even when the controls were set on exhaust. Their living room was air-conditioned, but Ralph and Lillian preferred to spend the hot summer hours on their back porch overlooking a shady yard. The screening was old and full of holes—"like me," Ralph said. The larger yard next door had been owned by an eccentric millionaire and did indeed have a homemade miniature golf course.
Lisa said, "Where's the killer cat?"
"Don't worry, he's there," Ralph said.
Lillian served tuna salad on the porch, and Lisa found herself actually enjoying food for the first time since she discovered her grandfather's mangled body. "What's the secret ingredient?" she asked.
Lillian said, "Chicken soup."
Ralph made stingers for dessert with plenty of shaved ice. Then he said, "I told the police lieutenant that you were staying here."
"Okay."
"You're still determined to play detective."
"I'm not playing."
"But you don't know where to begin."
"Meg Webster was sent away by her family because she wanted to tell me something."
"If that's true, then maybe your first step is to go to the Adirondacks and find out."
Lisa nodded. "Maybe."

"At least write to her."

"I think maybe she doesn't want to put it down on paper. Otherwise she would have sent me a note by now."

"That makes sense. Maybe you're a good detective after all." Ralph stirred in his captain's chair, making it squeak. "Okay, that's a possible line of inquiry. But there's another one. Maybe the killer is sending you messages."

Lisa had been given the best seat on the porch— an outdoor chaise longue. She sat forward. "You mean like the little lamb?"

"I mean like the little lamb, I mean like your father's kid gloves and his ski mask. I mean like the knitting needles and the ball of wool in that woman's room. And what was it that you found on your grandfather's floor, his diploma from Cornell, right?"

Lisa stared at him. "So what's the message?"

"Let's think about it," Ralph said. "There's the lamb, nothing subtle about that. There's the kid gloves. You know what a kid is?"

Lillian answered. "That's a little lamb, isn't it?"

"Right. And what was the ski mask made of?"

"Wool!" Lillian cried, as if she were on a TV game show eager to answer before the other contestants. "Just like the knitting needles and wool! But I don't get the diploma thing. How's that connected?"

"Uncle Shaky," Lisa said. "He didn't call it a diploma, he called it something to do with sheep."

Ralph nodded. "A sheepskin. That's what diplomas were written on in past centuries. So they were called sheepskins."

Lillian said, "That dog, wasn't he a sheep dog?"

"Right," Ralph said. "Give that woman a cigar. He was a sheep dog."

Lillian clapped her hands and beamed at her cleverness.

Lisa stood up. "What time is it, Uncle Ralph?"

"A little after seven-thirty. Why?"

"I have to talk to Uncle Shaky. That's my grandfather's friend Tom Shakespeare. He wouldn't be in bed already, would he? I don't care if he is, I'll wake him up, damn it!"

Ralph said, "Now hold on, honey. You're not going anywhere without me. What's this about Shakespeare?"

But Lisa was already in the house heading for the front door. "Well, come on if you're coming! I'll tell you on the way."

Lillian was on the move. "Yeah, Ralph, let's go."

Since Lisa's Firebird was blocking Ralph's Rabbit in the driveway, they piled into her car. She screeched backward into Shore Road, nearly ramming the security patrol car that was standing there. She hollered, "Stay outa my way, Paulie! I don't need you goosing me from the rear."

She shot forward and was startled when Ralph's foot stretched over and jammed on the brakes. She glared at him, breathing heavily.

Ralph said quietly, "You survived a plane crash through luck—"

"Luck!"

"But that's no guarantee your luck will hold. You're going to drive sensibly or you're not going at all."

She snorted. "Old people!"

Lillian cried from the cramped backseat, "Who's old?"

109

Ralph said, "Old or young, are you going to drive carefully?"

After a moment Lisa said meekly, "Yes, Uncle Ralph." She noticed a concerned Paul Doran standing by her open window. "Get lost, Paulie," she said. Turning back to Ralph, she said, "If you'll be so kind as to take your damn foot off the brake . . ."

She drove with excessive slowness the rest of the way to her grandfather's house in Little Neck. The last time she had been there had been with her father, and memories pressed in.

She leaped out of the car. "Come on, you old people," she said.

Lillian muttered, "Whippersnapper."

Lisa let them in with her key and headed toward the staircase, calling, "Uncle Shaky," then noticed that the light was on in her grandfather's examining room. She veered across the waiting room and into the lighted office.

Tom Shakespeare was seated on the old veterinarian's barstool with his forearms on the table, his head drooping, his face a deathly white. A string of saliva hung from slack lips. The table was littered with nondescript papers as though a wastebasket had been emptied on it.

Lisa sprang to his side, put a hand on his neck, and said his name. He moved his head but didn't raise it.

"Sugar," she exclaimed. She ran back through the waiting room and up the stairs. A moment later she clumped back down with her grandfather's sugar bowl. She shoved a spoonful into the old man's mouth, most of it landing on the table. She shoved another spoonful into the mouth.

The reaction was startlingly swift. In less than a minute the bulky old man straightened on the stool and peered at her blearily. "My niece-a Lisa," he muttered.

"You forgot your shot again," she said sternly. Then she snorted. "Old people!"

Ralph said, "That was amazing. How'd you know he was in insulin shock?"

"I saw Gramps do it once," she said. "The old dope keeps forgetting he gave himself a shot and gives himself another." She turned to Shakespeare. "How're you doing, Dopey?" she asked, but she said it tenderly.

"Not so bad for an old dope," he said. "Did you bring a doughnut? I could use a doughnut right now." Lisa shook her head in exasperation. The man really shouldn't be living alone. She determined to hire a nurse to look in on him every day and make sure he was all right. After all, if she was rich, what better way to spend her money?

Ralph said, "I think we ought to get him upstairs."

Lisa said, "In a minute." She flicked a hand at the jumble of papers. "What's all this, Uncle Shaky?"

"Oh, that." Shakespeare waved vaguely at the cabinet behind him. "Bottom drawer," he said. "Just going through Homer's stuff. When he didn't know what to do with something he shoved it in there. Junk, all junk, why he kept it I'll never know."

Ralph was pawing through the papers. "Old receipts, drug company circulars, notices from Cornell, old postcards, nothing important . . . Let's get him upstairs, we can't leave him here."

The old man said, "Wait." There was a bewildered look on his face. "There was something. What was it now? Something funny." He lifted his arm. "Oh, yes. This."

It was a sheet of paper that had apparently been crumpled and then straightened out. With it was a crumpled envelope.

Lisa looked at the paper, saw handwriting, saw the words arbitrarily rearrange themselves. She handed it to Ralph Simmons. "What does it say, Uncle Ralph? Can you read this scribbling?"

Ralph saw that it was written in an unlettered hand but was quite legible. He knew of Lisa's disability and perused the letter without comment. "It's dated more than two years ago," he said. "From an address in Van Nuys, California."

"California!" Lisa exclaimed.

Ralph waited a moment, then read aloud:

Hey old buddy—
Youre a long way from the ranch at San Ignacio but nor far enough. You shoulda kep going to China so I couldnt ketch up. So now I caught up thanks to that magazine. Maybe theres a statue of limitations on the thieving you did but theres no statue of limitations on murder. Even after like 54 years, no sir. You could look it up.

No hard feelings but you owe me old buddy. When you took off with the whole boodle that wasnt a nice thing to do. You knew Id try to follow but Ill say this for you you were fast. Tricky too. I admire you for it— forget what happened at the Cheyenne fraight yard—I was mad you can understand that.

Im not mad anymore. I just want my money. Or someones gonna hear about the murders. Comprendo?

That magazine says youre now an angel of mercy. Listen Im not laughing but thats funny as hell. Ifn it makes you feel better think of it as showing mercy to

112

me. Lord know I need it. I had bad luck all my life thanks to you old buddy you bastard. I need the dough bad.

All I ask is my share. I leave the amt up to you. Not less than 50 thou. More ifn you have any sense of justiss.

Send it to me here. Ifn I dont get it in 2 weeks Ill know what to do. Get my drift?
    Your old buddy
    Luis San Sebastian

Lillian Simmons exclaimed, "Murder! What's this about murder?"

Ralph said, "A crude attempt at blackmail. The old doc obviously started to throw it away. I wonder why he kept it."

Tom Shakespeare said, "Maybe he thought he *had* thrown it away. I told you about that drawer."

Lisa said, "Read it again, Uncle Ralph. Slowly."

Ralph read it again.

Shakespeare said, "I thought it was just a crank letter. Maybe I ought to give it to the police."

Lisa took the paper and envelope from Ralph, saying, "I'll do it, Uncle Shaky. But let's get you upstairs. You're still a little dizzy, aren't you?"

"No more than usual," he said with a faint smile. "Last time I was like this Homer had to hire piano movers."

"Very funny," Lisa said. To Ralph Simmons she said, "I'll pull and you push, that ought to do it."

Shakespeare was laughing. He made it up the stairs on his own, with little help from front or rear.

When they had him settled on the sofa, Lisa sat in her grandfather's chair. She said, "Tell me again what

Gramps told you about California. He worked at a sheep ranch, right?"

Shakespeare spread his hands to indicate emptiness. "That's about all, sweetie. A sheep ranch."

"Did he say where?"

Shakespeare shook his head.

"How about this San Ignacio? Did he mention that?"

Shakespeare continued to shake his head. "But I looked it up in the atlas. It's way up north of Sacramento, up near Chico. That's where it is on the map, for all the good it does us."

"The sheep ranch was there."

"Could be. Probably was. Fifty-five years ago."

"He didn't say anything about a murder?"

"Lisa, I've told you all I remember!"

"That's where the money came from," Lisa said. "This shitepoke says Gramps stole it. Can anyone believe that?"

Lillian murmured, "Unbelievable!"

Shakespeare lowered his eyes. "All I can say is, well, he acted guilty about it." He raised his eyes to Lisa's. "Not that I believe Homer would steal anything. The crazy thing is this character wanted fifty thousand dollars from him. Homer didn't *have* that much, not without selling the house. Listen, Homer Honeywell was a living saint, I'll never believe otherwise."

They left a few minutes later, after Lisa had made the ailing man promise he would follow the nurse's orders when she came.

They were slumped once again on Ralph's back porch. A breeze was coming off the bay, and they were enjoying the pleasure of it.

Ralph told Lisa she was doing a nice thing in providing a nurse for Shakespeare.

She shrugged. "It's what Gramps would have wanted. It'll keep him free a while longer. I don't think Uncle Shaky'd do so good in a home."

"Are you going to give that letter to the lieutenant?" Ralph asked.

"He won't do anything about it," she said. "He doesn't think Gramps was murdered."

"Give it to him anyhow."

"Okay." She stood up. "I'm leaving for California tomorrow."

Ralph and Lillian gaped at her.

"There are things I have to find out," Lisa said. "Don't worry about me, I'll be okay."

Ralph stared a moment longer, then nodded. "Fine," he said. "I'll go with you."

Lisa tried to stare him down and couldn't. "If you want," she said. "But this is my thing, and I'm the boss."

Ralph said softly, "We'll see."

Ten

LISA LOOKED OUT the window of the Boeing 747 and said, "We're not going to land in *that!*" The air below had a sickly brownish tint as though seen through a dirty pane of glass.

Ralph said, "Welcome to Los Angeles."

"It looks like we could land *on* it, not in it."

"Once you're in it you don't even notice," he reassured her.

She said, "Uncle Ralph, I really don't want to stay with your son. I've got business to do."

"It's just a place to hang your hat. I promise that business comes first."

"I wanted to stay at the Beverly Hills Hotel."

"Why?"

"To see the movie stars."

"They don't live there. They're all out on location. Do you know how much it costs to stay at the Beverly Hills?"

"I've got money to burn."

"I don't," Ralph said.

The moving platform in the terminal struck her as being a flat escalator. "It's too damn slow," she said.
"We'll run after we get off it," Ralph said.
"What does your son do?"
"He writes television commercials."
"You mean like for Puppy Chow?"
"Like for Puppy Chow and armpit spray."
"Doesn't sound like much fun to me."

Waiting for their luggage to come down the chute, Ralph said, "See that man over there?"
"Yeah."
"He's a nobody. Everybody else is a movie star."
"You're very funny, Uncle Ralph."

She lost her temper at the Hertz car rental counter. They wouldn't rent her a car because she was under twenty-one. Before she could call anyone a shitepoke, Ralph Simmons nudged her aside and rented a car on his own credit card.
"A Firebird," she ordered.
"Okay."
"Red."
They had to settle for a blue one.
"I'm driving," she said.
"But I know Los Angeles, and you don't," he protested.
"So you be the co-pilot and tell me. Besides, I'm good at reading maps."
He spread the Hertz map on the counter. "Okay, find Van Nuys."
She found it.

"How would you get there from here?"

She showed him.

He made a face, handed her the keys. "So drive."

In the car he said, "Let's drop the bags off at Rob's first."

"Let's go to Van Nuys first," she said.

He sighed. "You're the driver."

Following the spaghetti trails on a map was one thing. Actually traversing them was another. She missed the entry ramp to the San Diego Freeway, and in trying to circle back, got lost in a maze of streets. Ralph murmured directions from the passenger seat.

At four-fifteen in the afternoon, the freeways were starting to clog. Spurting the Firebird into bumper-to-bumper traffic going sixty miles an hour, she grinned for the first time. "This is fun," she said, then found she was going south instead of north. Ralph instructed her on how to get off at Imperial, loop under the overpass, and get back on the freeway going north.

He said, "I'm glad Lillian didn't come."

"Why?"

"She'd have a heart attack with you driving."

"What's wrong with my driving?"

"You wriggle from lane to lane as if the car had hips. It doesn't."

"I know *that!*" she said, scooting into the fast lane.

Eventually they found themselves on Van Nuys Boulevard. "This isn't a freeway," Ralph said.

"So?"

"You're still doing sixty."

"God, what a nag!"

The address on the blackmail letter was a pink structure in the form of a U, enclosing a ratty garden, mostly dead. Sections of the stucco had crumbled away disclosing the underlying mesh. Occupying most of the left wing was a public house of some sort; an unlit neon sign declared it to be the "Guernica."

"Sounds like a disease," Lisa muttered.

They looked for a manager's office, and finding none, they went into the gloom of the public house. The bar area was deserted except for a skinny creature dressed in a matador get-up behind the bar, leaning on it with his elbows. He eyed them under lids at half-mast. Beyond the bar was a grand piano with empty barstools attending it, and beyond that an area of banquettes and tables. The only source of light was a ceiling spot illuminating a huge reproduction of Picasso's masterpiece that occupied most of the back wall. It was the first time Lisa had ever seen it, and she was shocked at the sight of horses screaming and women and children being dismembered.

"Nice cozy lounge," Ralph muttered.

Soft piano music lingered in the air like a subtle perfume, and Lisa noticed a man seated at the piano, somehow blending into it.

Ralph said to the stationary matador, "Where can I find the owner?"

The man shifted his eyes toward the piano player.

Ralph and Lisa moved to the piano and eased on to two of the stools. Lisa could now see that the player had a round rubicund face, tightly curled yellow hair with dark roots, lips that looked as if they had just eaten something delicious, and eyes that were steadily gleeful.

Lisa said, "Are you on coke?"

The man laughed, a strange gurgling laugh that made Lisa want to laugh, too.

"Good Lord, no," he said. "That would be too much. No, I'm intoxicated by life and music. What turns you on, darling?"

Lisa thought a moment, and said, "I sometimes have Seven-and-Seven. I don't drink much."

"Delightful! What's Seven-and-Seven?"

"You own a bar and you don't know?" she said. "It's Seagrams Seven and 7-Up. Sometimes I put ice cream in it."

"Delightful! Is that what you want now? I think we can get some ice cream."

Lisa said, "That would be nice."

He turned to Ralph. "And you, sir? Seven-and-Seven with IC?"

"God no," Ralph said. "Do you think the sleeping bull-fighter could whip up an extra dry martini with a twist? All of a sudden I need it badly."

"I think that's possible," the pianist said. He called, "Kevin!"

The matador suit was too big for the little guy and drooped like hand-me-downs on a youngest child. At the thought of a matador named Kevin, Ralph changed his order to a double martini. Kevin's face remained unresponsive as he listened to Lisa's specifications.

When the man shuffled away, Ralph introduced himself and Lisa, and the piano player said his name was Don Smollett. "Rhymes with wallet," he said.

Ralph said, "I'm curious about the painting."

Smollet turned toward the posterlike reproduction, his face beaming. 'Guernica.' I love it, don't you?"

"Oh, it's a great painting," Ralph said. "But is it really appropriate in a cocktail lounge? This *is* a cocktail lounge, isn't it?"

"Whatever you want to call it," Smollett said. "What should we have on the wall, cherubs kissing? Dancing nudes? Bubbling champagne glasses? I know a bar owner who plastered his walls with photographs of the Mohave Desert, on the theory that they'd make the customers thirsty and they'd drink more. It didn't work. Nobody wanted to go back there, any more than they'd want to go back to Death Valley. What he needed was an oasis with or without dancing nudes. See what I mean?"

"But 'Guernica'?"

The piano player turned to study the painting. "It's sort of shocking at first sight," he said. "But it's an erotic turn-on. Makes the guys horny as bulls. That and the cute little ditties I make up. His lover doesn't stand a chance, that lover's gonna get it good!" He gurgled in delight. "I mean, but good!"

Ralph said, "Sounds like S and M. Isn't that what they call it? S and M?"

"If that's their bag," Smollett said. "Do you want to hear one of my songs?"

The matador arrived with their drinks. Lisa's had an ice-cream float with a cherry on top. It looked like a breast. "Who gets the Shirley Temple?" he asked with a straight face.

"Enjoy," Smollet said, and launched into a smutty song that seemed to be titled "I'm Gonna Sit Right Down on It," interpolated with little leaps off the piano stool and licentious "whoops." When he finished, he beamed at them.

Ralph said, "Very clever."

Lisa said solemnly, "We're looking for Looie San Sebastian."

Smollett's smile faded. "Strange man," he said. "I hope you're not related to him. Incidentally, it's Lu-is, darling, not Looie. Turned out to be crazy. Tell me you're not related to him."

She said, "No, we're just looking for him."

Smollett nodded. "Good. You wouldn't want an uncle like him, believe me. He was the filthiest man I ever saw. He smelled! Didn't he smell, Kevin?"

"Who?" the matador replied from the bar.

"San Sebastian."

"He spit," Kevin said. "Had to get a spittoon just for him."

"Walking death," Smollett affirmed. "Got me in a bitchy lawsuit."

"Is he still here?" Lisa asked.

"No, he isn't, darling. I doubt if he's still alive. I never should have let him stay here that long, about a year, but then I'm like Will Rogers. I never met a man I didn't like. I felt sorry for him." He played sobbing music on the piano.

"There was the time two years ago when he came up with a suggestion that crazy me thought might go over. He said, Get somebody to do a sword dance, it fits in with the name of the place—Basque, you know—and I'd really have the place rocking. So that's what I did." He switched to De Falla's "Fire Dance."

"I got this Mexican kid and gave him a sword, and I played this thing—who knew the difference?—and the first night the clumsy kid missed on a leap and nearly cut his legs off. How did I know there was a bitchy lawyer in the place? He didn't even have to chase the ambulance. He knelt by the kid lying there in a pool of blood and signed him up."

He grimaced. "They're suing me for fifteen million dollars. You talk about S and M, that's S and M!"

Lisa said, "Where is he now?"

"The kid?"

"Mr. San Sebastian."

Smollett shook his head sadly. "The poor man finally went completely off his rocker. He became violent. He owed me five months' rent, but he kept saying he expected to come into an inheritance any day. I wasn't thinking straight. The old thing was seventy-five if he was a day, and whoever heard of anyone that old coming into an inheritance? When he left he still owed me eighteen hundred dollars, but it was good riddance, I was glad to get rid of him."

"You finally threw him out?" Ralph said.

"Had to, don't you know. He went berserk. He always hated the painting. Said it was a disgrace to his people. How he figured that I don't know. It was a minor atrocity committed by the Nazis in Spain. I'd cut off his credit at the bar, but Kevin let him booze up anyhow. Kevin felt sorry for him, too. That was a mistake, wasn't it, Kevin?"

The matador moved slightly in what was probably a shrug.

"What did he do?" Ralph asked.

"Oh God, it was wild," Smollett said. "He was staring at the painting, but he wasn't thinking erotic thoughts. Suddenly he let out an ungodly scream and attacked the painting like it was a man-eating lion. He had a long knife and slashed at it. Luckily the knife hit the brick wall behind it, and the blade broke." The pianist's face took on a stern look. "I couldn't let him stay after that."

Lisa said, "Where did he go?"

Smollett didn't seem to hear her. He said, "I took the lovely thing down from the wall and very carefully pasted it back together again from the back. If you get up close, you can still see the slash marks. Go ahead, see if you can find them."

Ralph said, "I believe you. It was a terrible thing to do, terrible. Do you know where he went when you kicked him out?"

Smollett made a face. "Cappy can tell you. He had been warning me about the crazy old bugger, said he was dangerous, and I didn't believe him until the night the bugger murdered 'Guernica.' So when he left, Cappy followed him to make sure he wasn't coming back. But your ice cream is melting, darling. Do you want a straw? It depresses me to talk about San Sebastian. Would you like to hear another of my songs? It's called 'Comin' Through the Rye.' "

Ralph said, "Stick to 'Stardust.' You're really a hell of a good piano player, do you know that?"

"Thank you," Smollett said.

Lisa said, "Who's Cappy?"

Smollett sighed. "I was afraid you were going to ask that, you have a one-track mind, darling. Do you remember a nose tackle for the Rams named Bill Blood? They called him Captain Blood because he was so deliciously violent."

Lisa said, "What's a nose tackle?"

Ralph said, "He made the Pro Bowl six straight years. What ever happened to him?"

Smollett said, "Watch." He put a hand under the keyboard, then started to count. "One, two, three, four, five, six—"

A giant of a man burst into the lounge from the rear and charged toward Ralph Simmons.

Smollett said quickly, "No sweat this time, old Kong. Just wanted to talk to you."

The man screeched to a halt, the picture of monumental bewilderment until he understood that his bouncing services weren't needed. He was a six-foot-five three-hundred-pounder with a bald head that glistened in the dim light, and puffy little eyes in a lumpy face. His jeans and T-shirt were too tight for his massive body. Lisa stared at the great muscles and mentally compared them to Greg's; she couldn't help herself, she wanted to feel them and barely refrained from reaching out.

Then the man spoke, and the desire vanished. The voice was tenor rather than baritone and somehow soft despite the scowl on the face. "What's the problem?" he said.

"Luis San Sebastian," Smollett said. "These poor souls are looking for him."

The scowl turned to a look of concern. "Don't do it, folks," he said. "For your own sake, don't do it. That old mother is bad news, leave him be. He don't look like much, weak as a kitten, but I had to bust his arm to get him off the picture. He's a dangerous old piece of shit, don't let him fool you."

Ralph assured him that he and Lisa understood.

Finally the big man, with a show of reluctance, gave them an address on Wilmington Avenue in the area of Los Angeles called Watts. Ralph wrote it down.

Lisa said, "Watts?"

Ralph, feeling giddy, said, "He's on second. I dunno's on third."

Lisa said, "Who?"

Ralph said, "He's on first." Then he said, "Sorry, it comes over me once in a while, the old Abbott and Costello syndrome."

Captain Blood had the bewildered look on his face again. He said to Smollett, "These two are as nutty as San Sebastian."

Ralph said, "That's a black area, isn't it? Why would a white man move there? San Sebastian *is* white, isn't he?"

"Basque," Blood said as if it were a distasteful color.

Lisa said, "Did he ever talk about being on a sheep ranch?"

Smollett hit a discordant chord. "Sheep ranch? You mean he was actually on a sheep ranch? We thought he was talking about prison. He made it sound like prison. How about that, Cappy?"

The huge man scowled. "I still say he was an ex-con. Rough trade, you can tell."

Lisa was studying the piano player. "What did he say about the sheep ranch?"

Ralph said, "We have to go, Lisa honey." He finished his drink.

Smollett said, "You don't want to know, darling. Mr. San Sebastian was a pervert. What he said was filth, isn't that right, Cappy?"

"Filth," Captain Blood agreed.

Smollett said, "Back to work. Here comes the happy throng."

Ralph looked at his watch. Five o'clock. "Happy hour?" he said.

Ralph nodded, smiling. "Happy hour. People will go for a bargain even if it's something they don't want. Toro, toro!"

Captain Blood said, "Oh," and retreated through the back door, presumably to get into a uniform.

Casually dressed people of all ages were entering, more men than women. They heard Smollett's piano music, and smiles slowly spread on their faces.

Ralph shoved a ten-dollar bill at the matador bartender, and they threaded their way out through the happy throng.

Outside he said, "Whew."

Lisa said, "Let's go to Watts."

Ralph said, "He's on second. We're going to Rob's, and I'm driving. We'll take the scenic route, down through Bel Air. Maybe we'll see a movie star walking his dog."

"Very funny," she said.

Eleven

SHE DIDN'T INTEND to be ungracious to Rob and Katie Simmons and their two kids, a boy seven and a girl nine. The trouble with them was there was nothing unusual about them, nothing that would bear out her image of Hollywood, no sophisticated talk, no glossy makeup, no elaborate practical jokes; Rob wasn't breathtakingly handsome, and Katie didn't wear a slinky dress. They were just like the people back home, except they lived in a nice apartment instead of a nice private house, and the kids played in a nice park across the street instead of down at the nice Savage Point dock. They lived in a place called Pacific Palisades. Nice. Besides, Lisa was exhausted.

She sat on the sofa with a blank look on her face. She heard Rob say to his father, "She's gorgeous," and she shrugged mentally. Her hearing was as good as her peripheral eyesight. She heard Katie's hushed voice in the kitchen: "She lost both her father and grandfather in less than a week! The poor kid!" And on cue, Lisa felt sorry for herself. The children steered clear of her.

Ralph didn't say much to her, either. He was busy horsing around with his grandchildren. Everything normal, soothing. Ralph told his son of their quest for San Sebastian.

Rob said, "Watts is perfectly safe these days, but it's probably smart not to go in there at night. There's always the chance of some poor bastard getting juiced up and looking for someone to take it out on." Then he and Ralph got into a serious discussion of the melting pot that didn't melt, and Lisa turned them off.

At nine she called Eddie Epstein collect at home. "Charge it to the estate," she said grandly.

He told her that the police now regarded the death of her grandfather as a possible homicide, and he was pressuring them to make a statement exonerating Shep, but they were afraid that he would sue the city for wrongful death. He sounded low in spirit.

She said, "He was a good dog."

Epstein said, "A prince among dogs."

The bedding arrangements were awkward. Lisa was given the girl's bedroom, and girl slept with the boy, and Ralph slept on the sofa. Lisa objected, but not too strenuously; she fell immediately into a deep sleep. She dreamt about Shep.

The rooming house was tucked between a bar and a laundromat, a three-story wooden structure with six steps leading to a modest stoop big enough to hold a canvas chair. The air was hot and poisonous. The teenagers on the sidewalk moved in slow motion. When Lisa parked the blue Firebird in front of the rooming house, the teenagers moved listlessly to inspect it.

Lisa and Ralph mounted the steps and introduced themselves to a gray-haired man sitting in the chair. He had the round flat face of a Mexican Indian, except that it was quite dark and withered. Though he was dressed in a blue work shirt and black corduroy pants, he sat with the benevolent ease of royalty on a throne.

He said his name was Fernando Cruz. He noticed Ralph's flushed face and labored breathing and asked politely if Ralph was suffering from asthma. Ralph said he never thought he had asthma until he hit L.A.

"It's not a city for people with bad lungs," the man said, nodding sympathetically. He spoke slowly and precisely with the barest trace of a Mexican accent.

"We're looking for one of your compatriots," Ralph said. "A man named Luis San Sebastian. We're told he moved here about a year ago."

The man laughed lightly. "No compatriot of mine," he said. "He said he was Mexican, and I let him in. He was no more Mexican than this pretty young lady. But he was in, and what could I do, I let him stay."

A raised voice from the sidewalk caused Ralph to look in that direction. Five teenagers seemed to be draped on the Firebird. "Is the car safe there?" he asked.

"Well, now," Cruz said, scratching his head. "Leave it there overnight and the piranha'll get it—you know, them vicious little fishies you see on television—leaving nothing but bare bones in the morning. I wouldn't like that. Dee-tracts from the values of my proper-tees."

"How about those kids?"

"Baby piranha," Cruz said. "They in love with a jazzy car, that's all. You leave anything valuable in there?"

"No, not really. It's a rental."

"Then you okay. They just looking and dreaming."

Lisa said, "Tell us about Mr. Sebastian. Is he still here?"

"Lordy no," the man said. "Sit on the top step there, young lady. You, too, gentleman. I'd ask you in, except it be wiser to stay out here and keep looking at your pretty car. Sometimes the dreaming get stronger than the looking."

Ralph sat down. Lisa remained standing.

Fernando Cruz settled back in his canvas chair. "Well, now, you asking about a very sick old man. Good for nothing, you might say. Way older than he should be. He *thought* old, not like me, I don't think old, I think *young*. How old do you judge me to be?"

"Hard to tell," Ralph said.

Lisa said, "Sixty?" and Ralph Simmons frowned at her.

Cruz slapped his knee. "Eighty-one! I own these three buildings, I'm working on my third wife, and I feel like one of those kids down there!"

"Hard to believe," Ralph said.

"Now this poor man you're looking for," Cruz went on, "he was seventy-five going on a hundred and five. He had one foot in the grave and four toes of the other foot. 'Course, he was sick, his lungs was rotting away, but that don't stop him from smoking, no siree. He one of those persons who born damn fools and stay that way for the rest of their lives. He smoke even when he cough up blood. I don't like to waste my sorrow on a man like that, but, well, I felt sorry for him just the same.

"Didn't have a pot to piss in, pardon my language, young lady, but he didn't. All he had was social insecurity coming once a month. I call it social insecurity cause he was getting the minimumest. Know what I mean by the minimumest? It's a word I made up. It means barely enough to pay for his cigarettes."

Cruz wagged his head sadly. "He had the brains of a wiggly worm. He had only one thing he could be proud of—he was white. Although sometimes I thought he looked a little yellow, but maybe that was just his liver rotting away. Anyways, he was white, by God, and I was a black bastard. That's what he called me, but it didn't bother me none. As I say, I was trying to feel sorry for him, and nothing the old rattlehead called me could hurt me none."

He nodded toward the kids on the sidewalk. "But calling those kids that, that's another matter. They don't understand about rattleheads. Well, one night they horsing around down there—their heads ain't exactly crammed with smarts, either—and along come Mr. White Man, and one of the kids bump into him accidentally on purpose. And this old crabapple we talking about, he say, 'Get outa my way, you black bastards.' And he spit.

"Well, the kids play with him after that. They don't realize they shouldn't play so rough with a old man going on a hundred and five, even if he asking for it. I watch for a minute, maybe two, but when I see blood coming out of this white man's mouth, I break up the party and get the po-lice to call a ambu-lance.

"And that's the last I see of Mr. Luis San Sebastian. I don't know if he living or dead. Don't matter to me none. A born damn fool and never learned better. I got better things to worry about than him." The sad shake of his head belied his words.

"But he was alive when they took him away?" Ralph said.

"If you call that living," Cruz said. "He was in a fix, you see. He had to cough up this blood or he gonna drown in it, but he act like one of his ribs is broke. You ever try to cough when you got a broken rib? Don't do it, that's all I can say."

Lisa said, "Where did they take him, Mr. Cruz?"

"Harbor General, young lady. I know that, 'cause the po-lice take his stuff there." He shifted his gaze from her to a point up the avenue. "Lemme ask you this. See that steely gray car up there, the one with the roof peeling off? Is that some person you know?"

Lisa peered at the car parked three hundred feet away and frowned. It was a full-size antique, possibly an old Cadillac. It looked vaguely familiar, even vaguely sinister in its battleship color. She shook her head. "Uncle Ralph?" she said.

"Nobody I know," he said.

Cruz called to one of the teenagers on the sidewalk. "Do-Right!"

The boy looked up at him.

Cruz said, "Do something for me, my man. See if you can help the person in the steely gray heap up there. Do you understand me, Do-Right?"

The kid half-grinned, then he and his four friends strolled toward the gray car.

"They're a frightening sight, ain't they?" Cruz said with a gleeful laugh.

"What's up?" Ralph asked.

"Nothing, Mr. Simmons, nothing excepting that old heap pulled in there just after you all stopped here. I'm a nosy old black bastard, and I kept my eye on it. Nobody got out. Then I thought maybe it be a friend of yours waiting to help in case of trouble. But you don't know him?"

"No," Ralph said.

"So maybe it just a coincidence—" he pronounced in *co-in-see-dence*—"and that mother ain't got nothing to do with you. We'll see."

The boys came abreast of the car and halted. Do-Right bent to peer in, and suddenly the car swerved from the curb and sped away. It turned left at the far intersection and disappeared.

Cruz slapped his thigh and chortled. "See!"

Ralph said slowly, "Of course, it doesn't prove he was tailing us—"

Lisa said, "Remember yesterday when we got on the freeway from the airport and I said, 'This is fun'? There was a car just like that one got on after us, you know scooting into traffic, and I thought, So everyone drives like that around here. Now I think maybe he was following us. Did you notice him, Uncle Ralph?"

Ralph said, "Sorry, honey. The only things I look for in the rearview mirror are cops' cars. All the others are just cars."

The boys strolled back to the sidewalk below them, and Do-Right reported to Cruz. "Two honky dudes just sitting there doing nothing. Didn't want no help."

"Thank you, Do-Right," the old man said.

Lisa said, "Is your real name Dwight?"

The kid grinned. "I like Do-Right, 'cause that's what I do." He imitated Kareem making a hook shot. "Maybe I change it legally." The other kids were guffawing, claiming that he missed and he ought to call himself Do-Wrong.

A few minutes later, having gotten directions to the hospital from the old man, they left. The last thing Cruz called down to them was, "I like your name, Miss Honeywell. It flow like molasses, tastes good."

Spinning down the freeway, Lisa kept an eye on the mirror, but traffic was heavy and every second car was gray, "steely gray." Ralph, too, kept turning in the passenger seat to look back.

"Do you see him?" she asked.

"Twelve times," he said. "Oops, here comes another."

"Why would anyone want to follow us?"

"If they are," Ralph said with a shrug, "could be they're car thieves with an order for a blue Firebird. I give up. Here's the exit to the hospital."

The dizziness hit Lisa as soon as she entered the hospital, and it enraged her. She leaned on Ralph for a moment, saying, "The smell, doesn't it make you want to puke?" He led her to a chair, but she refused to sit down. She said, "I'm beginning to hate this old San Sebastard. Let's get it over with, damn it."

They got the usual bureaucratic runaround, Ralph leading and she following. It was a walkaround really, leading to a starchy assistant administrator, who was disturbed by the fact that they were not relatives of the patient.

Ralph said, "Okay, he's my older brother. I just didn't want to admit it."

"I don't blame you," the administrator said. "I don't believe you, either. But I guess there's no harm in telling you that the patient was discharged to a nursing home for the indigent. Are you prepared to pay your brother's bill?"

"How much just for the name and location of the nursing home?" Ralph asked.

The administrator sighed. "That's the free part. It's the Holy Innocents Nursing Home." She wrote down the address of a slip of paper. "It's up near the airport. Do you know how to get there?"

"We'll find it," Ralph said.

He thanked her, and they left.

Riding north on the San Diego Freeway, Lisa said, "I hope he's still alive."

Ralph, who was driving, grumbled, "There are gray cars all around us."

"Any with two honky dudes in them?"

"They all have two honky dudes."

Lisa said, "If they want the damn car, let them have it. I'm hungry."

They got off the freeway near the airport and stopped at a taco stand for a snack. Lisa ordered a cheeseburger, and the man said they didn't serve cheeseburgers. Lisa cried, "This is still part of America, isn't it?"

Ralph induced her to try a taco.

Frowning, she ate her taco in silence.

Ralph said, "How was it?"

"I hated it," she said. "Let's go."

They were surrounded by gray cars driven by honky dudes as they searched for the Holy Innocents Nursing Home.

Twelve

THE NURSING HOME was a rambling one-story structure that had once been an innocent white in conformity with its original function as an orphanage but had now acquired a grimy gray surface in keeping with its present function as a warehouse for elderly discards. The grounds, enclosed by a rusted link fence, covered about three acres of arid land crossed by crumbling walkways, sporting a cement play area dominated by a dinosaurlike skeleton from which children's swings had once hung. A tired grove of what were probably orange trees stood, but barely, behind the building. The grayish monochrome blanketed everything, including the trees. The only other living thing in sight was a dog which, as they looked, lowered itself in the shade of a tree and played dead.

The first person they encountered inside the door was a squat woman in an orange uniform who didn't speak English. She led them to a harried-looking nun, who said, "We do the best we can under the circumstances." She said it crankily.

"I'm sure your efforts are heroic," Ralph said, and Lisa envied his ability to make the disarming comment without sounding sarcastic.

"San Sebastian, San Sebastian," the nun repeated, flipping impatiently through a card file. "Oh, yes, that one." She looked up at Ralph and Lisa. "I'm afraid you'll have to see him in his room. He's not able to make it to the visiting room." She glared at them. "He's dying, you know."

"We'll try not to disturb him too much," Ralph said. "He *is* able to talk, isn't he?"

"Oh, yes." She stood up. "It's very kind of you to visit him. We don't get many visitors here. He should be delighted to see you." She unconsciously stressed the "should," implying a doubt on her part.

She spoke a few words to the orange-clad attendant, then said, "Dolores will show you to his room. I hope you enjoy your visit." Again, the implication of doubt.

Following the squat person along a hallway painted institutional green, Ralph said, "From here the cemetery must look pretty inviting." His further words were lost in an onrushing roar that made the building quiver. When the roar receded, he murmured, "Ah, the joys of abiding near an international airport."

It was a small room with four beds in it, three of which were empty, their occupants presumably somewhere else in the building. Propped on the fourth bed was a figure that could only have been painted by El Greco at his most bizarre—spiky gray hair in wild disarray, thin face slightly distorted, black eyebrows over mad eyes that were fixed on the intruders, the rest of the figure lost in the institutional gown and gray sheet that entwined him—except that the great Spanish artist would have had a much richer palette than the dull grays and off-white of "San Sebastian on His Deathbed in Holy Innocents Nursing Home, City of the Angels, California." On the wall over the bed hung a plain wooden cross.

Ralph said, "Mr. San Sebastian?"

The voice that came from the bed was surprisingly strong. "I don't know you," it announced.

Lisa advanced toward the bed. "You knew my grandfather—"

Ralph put a restraining hand on her arm. "We've come to have a little talk with you—provided you're up to it, of course. May we sit down?"

The old man grunted. "If you can find someplace to plant it."

There was one chair in the room. Ralph pulled it close to the bed, offered it to Lisa, who shook her head, then sat on it himself. Lisa sat on the edge of the bed next to the old man's.

"I wouldn't do that, girlie," the man said. "The feller that lives there has this new form of VD that's killin' off the queers and pansies—"

Lisa quickly stood up, then defiantly eased back down.

The man started to speak but went into a coughing fit instead. He leaned on an elbow and spit into a receptacle on the floor. "Don't say I didn't warn you when your nose starts to fall off," he said. "Does anybody have a cigarette? I'm dyin' for a cigarette—"

"A good description," Ralph said.

"And my money's run out for the month."

"You say that guy's got AIDS," Ralph said. "What have you got?"

139

The old lips curled contemptuously. "They say I got cancer of the lungs and everything else. Bullshit! I just got bushwacked by a gang of mean niggers, busted a rib, that's what hurts, but I got a surprise for the black bastards—" He started coughing again just as another plane roared overhead, making speech impossible.

Ralph noted the face that flushed and the red dribble from the mouth, and muttered to himself, "So there's blood in the old boy yet."

Lisa heard him and said, "Not much."

When the coughing and spitting ended, she said, "About my grandfather—"

"That's the second time you mentioned him, girlie. Who the hell is your grandfather?"

"Homer Honeywell."

A range of emotions flitted across the ravaged face before settling on—what?—sardonic glee? "Well, I'll be screwed, blewed, and tatoo-ed!" he said. He scrambled to a sitting position against the headboard. "Yeah, that's right, that shit-eatin' magazine did say he had a granddotter. So you're it, eh? Who's this fat old geezer?"

"My Uncle Ralph," she said coldly. "And Mr. Smollett was right—"

"So you met that little fairy, isn't that nice."

"He said you had a filthy mouth. Somebody ought to wash it out with soap and water."

"By God, you sound like Homer! Come on like a mealy-mouth holy man, what'd that magazine call him—patron saint of dogs and cats, something like that—come on like a saint and all the time with murder and thievery in his heart. Why'd you come here, girlie?"

His face took on a crafty look. "It can't be you came here with money, thinkin' to buy me off? Well, the stinkin' old bastard took his sweet time—"

The roar of a plane drowned his words, and he shook a bony fist at the ceiling. When he could speak again, he seemed to have lost all energy, and his face had an eerie transparency as if he were fading into death before their eyes. "Where's the money, girlie?" he said.

Ralph Simmons said, "Before we get into any talk about that, old man, we have to make sure you're the right San Sebastian. After all, we're talking about something that happened more than fifty years ago. That's a reasonable thing for us to do, isn't it? Could be you heard the story from the real San Sebastian and are trying to cash in. It's been done before."

The old man smiled. "What d'ya want to know?"

"Your first name is Luis, right?"

"Luis, right."

"You wrote that extortion letter to him two years ago?"

"Extortion, what's that, extortion?"

"Trying to squeeze money out of him."

"Only askin' what's mine, that's all."

Ralph settled back in his chair and crossed his arms across his chest. "Okay, if you're the real San Sebastian, tell us what happened in San Ignacio back in nineteen thirty-one."

"You mean about this back-stabbin', bush-whackin' Honeywell?"

"Certainly about this back-stabbin', bush-whackin' Honeywell. Who else?"

"First tell me how much money you brought."

Ralph said, "First tell us about San Ignacio. If you don't, we'll know you're not the right San Sebastian, and we won't take up any more of your time."

The man settled back against the headboard and started to speak, sometimes strongly, sometimes faintly. His tale was disjointed, and Ralph had to interrupt frequently with questions, while Lisa stared in silence, held by the man's glittering eyes, not knowing whether the glitter was fired by malice, avarice, rage, remorse, or rebellion against the cruel designs of Fate. The session was prolonged by the man's painful coughing spells and the thunder of the planes overhead.

When it was finished, Ralph gave him two dollars and told him to buy a pack of cigarettes.

Later they went over his story and put it in proper sequence. For Lisa's sake, Ralph Simmons, who had been a boy at the time and remembered hazily the plight of his neighbors, filled in the background. "This was before the New Deal programs came into being," he said. Lisa looked at him blankly, and Ralph sighed.

It was the heart of the Great Depression, twelve million workers had lost their jobs and couldn't find other employment, their savings had vanished, and they faced starvation. Millions of men were on the move across America looking for work, any work, anywhere, no matter how menial or degrading, just to get a few dollars to feed themselves and, hopefully, their families.

Luis San Sebastian was one of the lucky ones, or so it seemed at the time. He had a trade of sorts and actually found employment in that trade, unlike lawyers who sold apples and teachers who dug ditches. His father was a Basque immigrant who had a small sheep ranch on poor land in Montana, and thus young Luis knew something of sheep herding. When the bank took away the San Sebastians' land the family scattered, and Luis trekked over the mountains to California. He found work as a herder on a larger sheep ranch in San Ignacio in the foothills of the Trinity Mountains in the northernmost reaches of the Sacramento Valley.

The family that owned the ranch was named Durango. The father was a hard-working man, shrewd and distrustful of banks. He was also a frugal man who parted with money sparingly. He gave Luis room and board and four dollars a week, more than enough to keep Luis in cigarettes but not nearly enough to provide the wine and women the wild young man craved.

The mother was a sturdy soul who had done her full share of herding until she had broken a leg that knitted poorly and left her with an incapacitating limp. The elder son Joaquin had been sent to live with relatives in another state while he went to college. The unschooled father had a great faith in education. Luis never met Joaquin. That left only the fifteen-year-old son Francisco to help with the sheep, and while he, too, was a hard worker like his father, there was just too much work for father and son to handle alone. Hence, their hiring of Luis and a short time later a non-Basque hobo named Homer Honeywell.

The two hired hands bunked down in what was little more than a shed about a hundred feet from the frame house in which the Durangos lived.

"I loved that family," San Sebastian told Ralph and Lisa. "They took me in when I was desperate, and I've always been grateful to them."

At first he and Homer got along well enough, but then Homer became a big pain in the ass. He complained. The Durangos had winterized the shed and put in a big pot-bellied stove, but Homer complained about the living quarters all the same: it wasn't up to the standards he had been used to, la-di-da. He hollered about the pay, four bucks a week. They got a fortune stashed away in that house, he grumbled; they're the only ones who didn't go down when the bank crashed, they got it all in that damn house, and they pay us like we're friggin' niggers.

Luis didn't know what Homer was getting at at first, but he finally realized that Homer was suggesting that he and Luis steal the money and run.

"Bull cookies," Lisa interjected. "My grandfather would never do a thing like that."

"That's what you think, girlie. He may a' been a meek lamb on the outside, but inside he was a slobbering wolf. Believe me, I know."

Anyhow, one night Luis was awakened by smoke and a flickering light. The Durangos' house was on fire. He dragged Homer out of his bunk, where Homer acted as if he were asleep, and they ran to the house to try to rescue the people inside. They smashed in the front door, and Homer searched the downstairs rooms while Luis dashed up the stairs toward the bedrooms. But the second floor was an inferno, and Luis barely made it outside before he collapsed. Then he became aware of his buddy Homer lugging a small metal chest from the house. He watched as Homer disappeared into the night.

The three Durangos were charred almost beyond recognition.

You have to understand that the ranch was high up the slopes, San Sebastian told Ralph and Lisa, many miles from the nearest humans, and as far as the two hired hands knew there was no law officer and certainly no undertaker in the hamlet of San Ignacio. There was no one for them to turn to, Homer said. Luis was still in a state of shock.

So the rattled young men dug three graves behind the smoldering ruins of the house, placed the bodies in them, and Luis said the words over them. He remembered what he said. He said, "Agnes Day, that's Lamb of God." He said, "Lamb of God, these were good people, have mercy on them. *Requiescat in pace,* that's rest in peace, in case you don't know what the hell it means." Then he said, "Adios, amigos." And he wept.

(Lisa had difficulty picturing this surly old man weeping.)

After the burial the full realization of their plight hit them. They were unemployed once again, they had a large flock of sheep on their hands which they couldn't possibly take care of by themselves, and winter was approaching. The only survivor of the family was Joaquin, but he was far away, living with unknown relatives and attending an unknown college. And they knew the family had no bank account. There was no bank.

As if to ram home the impossible situation they were in, the first light snow of the season began falling. That day they took the sheep out to graze, but they knew they had to do something quickly to resolve the situation. They sat on their bunks and discussed it.

While they were sitting there, the kerosene lamp guttered and died. Where's the damn kerosene, Luis asked Homer, and Homer said, It's all gone. Then Luis remembered the odor he had smelled in the flaming house, and he knew that the fire was not an accident but had been deliberately set by Homer Honeywell. He remembered something else. When he had awakened Homer, Homer was fully dressed!

They sat in the darkness, and for the first time Luis was frightened. What would one more murder mean to a man who had already murdered three? Luis grabbed his blanket and slept outdoors that night.

He slept very poorly, and at the first light of dawn he saw Homer leave the bunkhouse and steal off to a stand of trees that bordered a shallow ravine. He didn't dare follow in the open, but when Homer went back to the bunkhouse, Luis made his way to the trees and saw where Homer had hidden the metal strongbox. He looked in the box and saw more money than he had ever seen before, also some jewelry and the deed to the land. He closed the lid without disturbing the contents.

He didn't know what to do, he just knew he had to keep his knowledge from Homer or he would wind up dead. He went back to Homer and said it was plain that they had to move on but they couldn't leave the sheep untended to die in the coming winter.

And Homer said, Remember that feller with a beard who Durango threw off the land, well, that feller thought Durango had sunk with the bank and offered to buy the sheep from him at ten cents on the dollar. Homer said the only thing to do that he could think of was to find this feller and sell the sheep to him, that way the sheep wouldn't be a total loss. He told Luis to stay with the sheep, and he would go find this feller and make the sale.

Luis didn't like the idea, but he knew that Homer would come back because Homer wouldn't skip off without taking the strongbox with him.

Three days later Homer came back with a large wad of money and a bottle of wine. He also had something else—a shotgun. He said they needed the shotgun to protect the sheep from wolves since the old shotgun had burned up in the fire. Luis figured he knew what the gun was really for, but he didn't say anything.

The feller with the beard was going to take possession of the sheep the next day. Meanwhile Homer disappeared into the trees with the money, obviously to put it with the rest of the valuables in the strongbox.

Luis bided his time, hoping to get hold of the metal box and escape, and somehow get the money into the hands of the absent Joaquin Durango, the rightful owner.

("Of course," Ralph said.)

That night Homer Honeywell was in a good mood, as if he had something to celebrate. He drank wine by candlelight and even offered some to Luis. He said he was going to share the money with Luis out of the goodness of his heart, but Luis didn't believe him. Homer fell into a deep sleep, but Luis stayed awake all night. Homer slept with the shotgun by his side, and Luis didn't dare try to snatch it from him.

As soon as it got light in the morning, Luis sneaked out of the bunkhouse, made his way to the ravine, and took the strongbox with him. He stuck out across rough terrain, joined the rutted road well below the ranch buildings. He was free, he thought, as he hastened down the road. Homer Honeywell had gotten himself drunk and was still sleeping it off. That's what he thought.

He came to a stand of pines, and Homer Honeywell was plunked in the road in front of him, with the shotgun trained on Luis.

"Nice mornin' for a walk, old buddy," Honeywell said. That's what they had called each other. Old buddy.

Honeywell told Luis to put down the strongbox. Luis placed it on the ground.

Then Honeywell said, "Start runnin'."

Luis begged Honeywell not to shoot.

Honeywell said, "Maybe you can outrun the shots, this thing's gonna go off in five seconds."

Luis turned and raced into the trees. The first blast went over his head. Honeywell laughed. In his panic Luis tripped and fell just as the second blast tore over his head, where his body would have been but for the fall. He scrambled into the trees and ran until he could run no more.

Then he was lost in a wooded wilderness, and it took him two days to find his way back to the valley. He remembered Honeywell's laugh and vowed to get revenge. All he knew about Honeywell, however, was that he came from somewhere in the East, and Luis reckoned that his former buddy would head in that direction—undoubtedly by train.

The murderous thief had a two-day head start, but he had to get down to Sacramento to catch the train, and he had to travel cautiously so as not to call attention to himself. Luis got lucky—the last piece of luck in his while life, he claimed—and got a ride all the way down the valley in the car of a traveling salesman, who was selling notions, whatever they were.

Having no money, Luis rode the boxcars as far as Cheyenne. He didn't know how it happened, but he caught up with Honeywell in the Cheyenne freight yard.

This time it was Honeywell who ran, because he had ditched the shotgun and didn't have a weapon. Luis San Sebastian had a knife. With all the frustrations building up in him, Luis was almost insane with rage, and he admitted that he attacked Homer Honeywell with the knife and probably would have killed him if he could.

But luck had deserted him. Honeywell, by chance, put his hands on a crowbar and bashed San Sebastian in the head.

That was the last time Luis San Sebastian had set eyes on Homer Honeywell until he saw Honeywell's picture in *People* magazine two years ago.

Lisa was still mesmerized by the eroded, self-pitying face. Ralph Simmons turned his gaze to the window, to the nearby grove of orange trees that bore no fruit and thought it an appropriate setting for this gnarled old man, who was as barren as the trees.

San Sebastian tried to continue the tale of his luckless life cursed by a thieving varmit named Homer Honeywell, but Ralph and Lisa had heard enough.

Ralph asked him when was the last time he had been to the East Coast, and the man said he had never been east of St. Louis. And Ralph believed him.

When Ralph gave him the two dollars, the man started to roar curses, then began coughing in a violent way.

They left as he was bent over the side of the bed expectorating blood.

Thirteen

"BULL COOKIES," Lisa kept saying until Ralph asked her to try another expression. When she did, Ralph shuddered and asked her to go back to "bull cookies." She insisted that San Sebastian's story was a lie from beginning to end. Well, not completely. The man obviously had known her grandfather all those years ago, and his incredible tale did account for young Honeywell's possession of a fortune when he returned from California.

They were sitting in Rob and Kate's living room after dinner, and the kids were watching TV in the boy's room. Rob and Kate listened sympathetically without breaking in.

"The man is bugs, out of his skull," Lisa said, glaring at Ralph. "Can you believe that pack of lies?"

"I don't necessarily buy his story," Ralph said, leaning forward with his forearms on his knees, returning her gaze. "Certainly not the implication of murder. But you have to understand what poverty can do to the most honest of people. Call it a case of temporary insanity.

It's conceivable—remember I'm only saying *conceivable*—that your grandfather did take the money, and when he got home and came to his senses, he felt terribly guilty, that's what Shakespeare said, he acted guilty—"

Rob Simmons piped up. "Macbeth?" he asked in a puzzled tone.

"Not that Shakespeare," Ralph said. "Homer's friend Tom Shakespeare said he acted guilty. Not only that, Honeywell got rid of the money as soon as he could. He put it into a trust for his son. That was Lisa's father. He didn't want to have anything to do with it. So, about the theft, all I'm saying is that the story is not inconceivable."

"Bull cookies," Lisa said. "Don't you think it's also possible that this old shitepoke is the one who killed Gramps? He hated him, he told us that, but he didn't know where to find him until two years ago when he saw that magazine. He sent the letter, and when that didn't work he started boiling, so he finally came east and killed Gramps the way you kill a pig—it's the way they kill sheep, too, isn't it?"

"I wouldn't know," Ralph said.

Lisa jumped to her feet. "Damn it, the whole thing points to San Sebastian! He was a shepherd, and he picked on old Shep to blame it on. It's that crazy old man who did it all!"

"Probably not," Ralph said quietly.

"What do you mean probably not? It's as plain as—"

"Can you honestly believe that that dying old man got out of bed, traveled three thousand miles to kill the man who brought him all that bad luck, and then crossed the country again and got back in bed?"

"Yes!"

"He was probably in that old folks' home all the time."

"We don't know that! We don't know when he went there from the hospital. We didn't get the date, did we? And even if he was there there's nothing to say that he didn't check himself out for a week or two and then go back in. We didn't ask that, did we? And the sister didn't say he was there *all* the time, did she? We have to go back there and find out. Are you coming?"

Ralph sighed wearily. "It's too late, honey, it's ten-thirty. That nun would be mad as a hornet if we woke her up to ask her questions. Besides, this man San Sebastian wouldn't have known about your father's secretary and—"

Lisa interrupted him. "What time did that sister say they got the old people up in the morning? She said six-thirty, didn't she? Wasn't it six-thirty?"

"Six-thirty, but—"

Lisa turned away from him. "I'm gonna be there at six-thirty, whether you're coming or not. I'm going to bed."

Ralph peered over at his son with a what're-you-gonna-do gesture. "There's more than one crazy person around here," he muttered.

She knew that Ralph was probably right. The old man couldn't be the killer, but she couldn't let the story just lie there unchallenged. Maybe he got someone to do it for him. If he didn't, maybe he knows who did. The trouble was, whatever he said was probably a lie even if it was the truth. Maybe they could force the truth out of him. Maybe if they got a priest, she thought craftily, a Spanish priest, and made the old man go to confession . . .

She squirmed in bed. God, it was a long time to six-thirty. She had been in bed only ten minutes.

Ralph Simmons stuck his head in the door. "Listen, honey, we'll make some telephone calls in the morning. To San Ignacio—they probably have a police force by this time. We'll find out what the records say."

"Good idea, Uncle Ralph," she mumbled. "After we go to that old folks' orphanage."

Ralph sighed. "Sleep tight," he said.

She didn't sleep tight at all. She was restless all night. At five, she was ordering the sun to rise. At six, she and a groggy Ralph Simmons were on their way through swirling early-morning mists that made everything seem muted and unreal.

They saw the same nun. She was in a cheerier mood than she had been the previous afternoon or probably would be later in this day. She did scowl at their request for further information about Luis San Sebastian.

"I told you the man is dying. He couldn't possibly go across the street much less across the country. He came here four months ago and has been here ever since—without leave. Does that answer your questions?"

"Are you a mother superior?" Lisa asked.

"Just plain sister," the nun said with a faint smile.

"Can we talk to him again?"

The scowl started to reappear, when a young woman in white broke into the office and spoke urgently in Spanish.

The nun's face took on a puzzled look, then she turned back to Ralph and Lisa. "It appears that I was wrong," she said. "Felicia tells me that your Mr. San Sebastian has gone AWOL. He is not in his room."

The young woman spoke again, and the nun rose to her feet. "Excuse me," she said. "There seems to be something wrong with the other residents in the room."

She left the office and marched starchily down the hall with the white-clad aide. Ralph and Lisa followed, unbidden and unnoticed. Lisa had the uneasy feeling she had had as a schoolgirl walking down a similar corridor to the principal's office.

The three men were still in their beds; one was groaning, one was sitting up with his head in his hands, and the third was lying flat on his back. The aide pointed to the head of the one who was sitting up. *"Sangre,"* she said.

"Yes, blood," the nun said. She glanced around and said, "I can't believe it. The man didn't have the strength to do this—to get out of bed and strike his roommates on the head and then leave. I would have said it was impossible." She was talking to herself rather than to anyone around her.

"Stir crazy," Ralph murmured.

"Yes, it's possible," the nun said to herself. "I've heard of that."

She gave orders to the aide, who scurried out of the room. Then she went into the bathroom for water to tend to the wounded heads.

Lisa peered around in puzzlement. San Sebastian's bed had obviously been slept in but was now empty. The three old men were clad in hospital gowns like the one San Sebastian had been wearing the previous day. She saw they were pale blue, not gray as she had thought.

Her eyes panned across the open window, took in the dusty orange grove that grew, or had stopped growing, about twenty-five feet away, swathed in mist like the valley of the shadow of death. She shuddered and pulled her eyes away.

A glimpse of pale blue.

Her eyes roved on—to the unmoving one in bed who looked like he was dead, to the nun who now with her sleeves rolled up was gently washing the crusted blood from the head of one of the others, her mouth soundlessly forming the word "Ooh" . . .

Ralph muttered, "Not much we can do here."

The store detective notices the whisper of blue beneath the hem of the shoplifter's dress, touches the woman on the arm, and the shoplifter runs. The store detective notices the touch of misty blue in the dark green leaves of the orange grove and senses that it doesn't belong there . . .

Ralph started to mutter something else, but Lisa had vanished. He frowned. He knew that Lisa had once been a candy-striper at North Shore Hospital and wasn't likely to be spooked by the sight of a little blood. He started to leave the room when movement outside the window drew his eyes—Lisa walking cautiously toward the trees.

She's flipped, he thought. He hastened into the hall, found the rear door, and followed her path to the trees. *I'm dreaming,* he thought, *I'm in a fog, I'm trying to catch up to my crazy substitute granddaughter, who is leading me into a dying orange grove. I don't really want to go, but it's my damned duty to stick close . . . just in case.*

She had come to a halt, staring. He caught up, gaped at the sight, and said, "Oh, God!"

The gaunt figure of what had once been Luis San Sebastian was hanging from a limb of one of the trees. Not exactly hanging, for the tree wasn't tall enough for a proper hanging, and the dead man's feet were on the ground. Yet there was an unmistakable hangman's noose around his neck. The look on the tortured face, with eyes bulging, seemed to testify that the old sheepherder had been given a vivid glimpse of hell before he died of strangulation, not by the noose but by cruel human hands.

Lisa shuddered violently. He put his arm around her shoulder and turned her away. "Nothing we can do for the poor bastard," he said.

He started to lead her toward the building, but she dug in her heels. "We have to tell them, honey," he said.

"No!"

"Okay, I'll do it," he said. "You head for the car." He pointed her toward the parking area.

She grabbed his arm. The building was almost completely hidden from their sight by the foliage. "You can't do that," she said. "We have to get the hell out of here! *Now,* before we're seen."

She tugged at him.

Ralph said it was their duty, and she said something vulgar about what he could do with his duty.

"We can't do this to my grandfather," she said.

Bewildered, he let her pull him through the trees toward the car.

"Get in," she commanded, and slowly he obeyed, willing to hear her nutty reasoning before he went back and reported the whereabouts of the missing patient.

She drove quickly away. "Good, nobody saw us," she said.

A short distance away, Ralph ordered her to stop. She pulled to the side of the road.

"Okay, why are we sneaking away like thieves?" she said.

After a moment she turned to him. He had never seen her eyes so ablaze with emotion.

"That was obviously not a suicide, right?" she said.

"It's kind of hard to picture a man hanging himself with his feet on the ground, right," he said.

"And it wasn't an accident."

"Hardly."

"So it was murder."

"Probably."

"That means the police."

He said, "So it means the police. Their curiosity is generally aroused by a murder."

She gave a grunt of exasperation. "Uncle Ralph, I *know* the police. We deal with them nearly every day at the store. They ask questions. Like, Why did you come to visit Mr. San Sebastian? If we lie, we're in trouble. If we tell them just a little bit, they want to know the rest. Sooner or later we'd have to tell them about the letter, and then we'd have to tell them what the old shitepoke said, that pack of lies about Gramps. We could make up a different story, but I'm a stinking liar, I found that out when I used to try with my mother and father. How good a liar are you, Uncle Ralph?"

Ralph grinned. "I wrote great advertising copy in my day. But this kind of lying? I'm a lazy man, honey, and I found out it's easier to tell the truth than to make a lousy lie stick. What's wrong with the truth?"

"Because in this case, damn it, the truth is a lie about my grandfather! Gramps was a mass murderer, a—an arsonist—that's right, arsonist?—a thief, and a rustler of sheep. And no matter what we say, that story is going to get in the newspapers, and it's going to be printed in the New York papers, and there goes Gramps's reputation." She glared belligerently at Ralph. "I'm not going to let that happen!"

"That's not necessarily going to happen," he said. "Besides, it may have a bearing on the murders back home."

"Bull cookies! Something that happened that long ago, no way, José! That old fart made enemies wherever he went, and his death is good riddance. Bringing my grandfather into it isn't going to help the cops, it's only going to waste their time and kill Gramps all over again." Tears filled her eyes.

Ralph said, "Still—"

"Still nothing! Listen, Uncle Ralph, I bet that sister doesn't know we followed her into the room, she was too busy worrying about the cracked heads. Not only that, she doesn't know our names. She didn't ask us, did she? So even if she tells the police about us, they wouldn't know where to look for us. So you don't have to worry about getting in trouble with the cops."

She put her hand on the gearshift.

"Anyhow, that's the way it's going to be. If you want to get out here and walk back, go ahead and do it. This car is running away."

She waited. An airplane roared overhead. Ralph Simmons remained seated in the passenger seat. She shifted into drive and took off.

When they were once again on the San Diego Freeway he glanced sideways at her. "You must be one hell of a store detective," he said.

"Damn right," she said.

Back at his son's home, Ralph made several telephone calls to police departments in San Ignacio, Redding, and nearby towns in Northern California. There was no record of the Durango deaths.

It was only midmorning, but they were sprawled on the son's sofa. Rob was at work, and Katie had made them coffee which was in mugs on the cocktail table before them.

"That seems to be the end of it," Ralph said. "Unless you want to go up to San Ignacio and nose around."

"Do you think we could find out anything?"

"Not a thing. Nineteen thirty-one seems to be prehistory in that neck of the woods. It's making me feel very old."

A short while later, Lisa said, "Why string him up, Uncle Ralph? Why not just kill him and let it go at that?"

"The Code of the West," Ralph said. "When ranchers caught up with cattle rustlers they hanged them from a tree, probably to make it look like a formal execution rather than vigilante justice. That made it seem legal."

Lisa thought for a while, and said, "It sorta fits, doesn't it?"

Ralph nodded. "Sort of."

That night they took the red-eye back to New York. In midflight somewhere high over the Mississippi watershed, Ralph stirred, glanced at the sleeping figure beside him, and saw that Lisa was curled up like an infant, her thumb in her mouth. He was deeply moved: this tough young woman who had dragged him across the continent in the quest for a killer was still a child, a killer's target in terrible need of infant comforts.

He vowed to protect her but doubted that he could.

Fourteen

LISA STAYED IN the Simmons's house for four days.

The first day she lazed on the back porch and counted the rips in the rusted screening. Ralph told her she had jet lag, but he knew it was more than that, a period of healing after a series of emotional wounds. Greg Muldavin came that evening, held her in his arms, and suggested that what she needed was for him to take her up to the spare bedroom she was using and put her to bed.

They were on the dark back porch. Ralph and Lillian were in the living room watching an old Cary Grant movie.

"Not here," she said, shocked. "Aunt Lillian wouldn't like it."

"Whatever you say, sweetie," he said. "When are you going home?"

"Honestly, that's all you think of," she said.

"There are worse things," he said, chortling like an idiot.

She felt so much older than this randy sweetheart of hers.

"Grow up," she said. "What's that hard thing in your pocket?"

"Something for you." He took a small handgun from his pocket and held it out to her. "Just in case you need it."

She refused to take it. "You have a thing about guns and knives, Gregory, and I don't like it," she scolded. He looked so hurt that she added: "It's just that guns give me the creeps. With the police and Uncle Ralph and you and Paulie Doran watching over me, I feel—"

"Paulie!" Greg said. "Is that pest still bothering you? Lemme talk to him, I'll—"

"Oh, stop it. He makes me feel safe."

"Safe from the killer maybe but not from him. Don't let him get near you, damn it, I know what he's after!"

"Don't worry, I can handle Paulie," she said.

"Famous last words," he growled.

The next day the restlessness returned. Her mother phoned and tried to insist that she come to Manhattan and live with her. "You're still my little girl," the mother said.

Lisa told her she wasn't coming and hung up. The call increased her tension.

Nothing was happening.

She drove to her grandfather's house to visit with Gramps's old friend Tom Shakespeare. His health was obviously failing, and his disposition with it. He complained about the nurse, he moaned and groaned about a variety of aches and pains, and Lisa realized his biggest problem was loneliness. She couldn't keep Uncle Shaky in the house too much longer or the lack of stimulation would kill him.

"Oh, by the way," he said, "I found this."

He held out a long key, which she recognized as a safe-deposit key.

She frowned at it. "Didn't Uncle Eddie collect all of Gramps's papers and stuff? He's handling it now that Pops is gone."

"He must have missed this, it was in an old coffee can along with stray nuts and bolts and pencil stubs and whatnot, even an old eyebrow tweezer. Epstein's a busy man these days, but I'm sure he'd have come looking for it when he saw payments for it in the checkbook."

Lisa took the key and said she'd give it to Epstein.

She asked the old man what he was doing for kicks these days, and he said with a wry smile, "Getting out of bed, that's an adventure for me every morning, and then there's food, glorious food."

She said, "Too bad you have nobody to talk to anymore."

"Oh, I talk to myself," he said. "The trouble is, I've heard all my stories before."

"Isn't there someone you'd like to come live with you?"

"Sophia Loren," he said. "But she has other plans."

"How about a dog?"

"Only if he can do the laundry. Seriously, I've been thinking about a dog, but—"

"Big or small?"

"Big enough to take a saddle so I can ride him up the stairs."

He was refusing to be serious, and that was a good thing, Lisa thought. She had found him morose and left him feeling silly. Since she had that effect on him, she knew she was elected to visit him as often as she could.

Epstein said on the phone, "When I couldn't find the key, I arranged for the bank to open it without his key. But it has to be in the presence of a state tax man. We have an appointment for the day after tomorrow. You don't have to be there, but you're welcome to come if you want to."

Lisa said she would like that.

In the afternoon she and the Simmonses went out on the boat with its new windows, and Lisa trolled off the rear. It amused her to tie the fishing line to her big toe, so she could lie in the sun and still fish like Huck Finn on his raft.

Ralph said, "If you catch a shark, he'll snip that toe right off."

"Let him," she said. "I have nine others, I'm loaded with toes." She was watching a cloud slowly changing from a white poodle to the Pillsbury dough boy.

He said, "I talked to Lieutenant Carbine."

She said, "Aren't you supposed to be steering this thing?"

"Lillian's becoming a master pilot. She's doing great."

"Then how come you don't let her dock it?"

"She's like you. She thinks the boat has hips."

"What'd the lieutenant say?"

"They haven't found the rifle yet. They're still looking. I told him about San Sebastian."

Lisa sat up. "How much did you tell him?"

"Just that the son of a Basque knew Homer Honeywell more than fifty years ago and he bore a grudge against him. And that he was murdered."

"That all?"

"I told him San Sebastian might possibly have a relative in the area."

"Like who?"

"Like nobody. I just thought I had to tell him."

"What did he say?"

"He didn't think it was important but he'd keep it in mind."

Lisa was silent for a minute. "He's going to ask more questions, you know that," she stated.

"If he thinks there's a connection, yes. Right now he doesn't."

She untied her toe and pulled in the line. "Uncle Ralph, I know you had to do it, and I'm glad you didn't tell him those lies about Gramps, but that damn policeman is gonna do more than keep it in mind. He has no other leads, so he's gonna be around asking his questions, and we're gonna be in the soup. Thanks a lot!"

She maintained a cold silence all the way back to the bay. As they were anchoring, she glanced at her house on Shore Road and saw a Chevy Nova in the driveway.

"I know that car," she said. "It's Meg's!"

It took twenty minutes for the launch to come and transport them to shore. The house was out of sight from there. She ran up the dock praying that Meg would stay put for another five minutes; she ran up Shore Road, around a curve, and saw the Nova coming toward her.

Meg pulled to the side, and Lisa got in.

Lisa said, "So you're back. How's that dumb lake?"

Meg looked around nervously. "I'm not supposed to be here. My folks think I'm still up at the lake. Where the heck have you been, darn it? I kept trying to call you. I thought something might have happened to you."

The last syllable quavered, and Meg started to cry. "Gee, it's good to see you," she said. "Alive," she added.

Lisa embraced her awkwardly. Meg seemed chubbier than ever. Her flesh felt cool and rubbery.

"Let's get away from here," Meg said. "I don't want to be seen."

"Your folks?"

"They don't want me talking to you."

As Meg drove away from Shore Road, Lisa saw the defiant set to her face. She said, "Why don't you tell your parents to go jump in the lake—what's the name of this stupid lake again, I never can remember it."

"Takamooga."

Meg drove south on Savage Point Parkway, across Northern Boulevard, and stopped on a side street. She said, "Someday I will, but I have to get through college first."

Lisa said, "Don't worry about money, I got loads. Tell them to go to hell."

"I can't," Meg said, and she cried again.

After a minute, Lisa said, "So what else is new?"

Looking away from Lisa, Meg said, "I took the rifle up to the lake with me."

"You mean—you mean the one that—"

"It was Brucie. You know how he gets. Sometimes I think he's crazy—my own brother! Mother and Daddy always took his side, they wouldn't believe about the crack and all. They thought he was just being a little wild like boys are supposed to be, and by the time he goes into Daddy's business he'll be all right. But he's worse than ever, he's stealing from them now, and they know it. They finally found out about the drugs, and the crazy thing is, my father blames your father!"

Lisa gave an incredulous laugh.

"You don't know my father," Meg said. "He was bugging your father to pass a law that kids in school should be tested for drugs. He wanted a tough law, but your father said he was against the mandatory part. Daddy knows now that Brucie's been on drugs all along, and he claims that if they had found out about it in high school they could have done something about it. I said to him it's Brucie's own fault not Mr. Honeywell's, but my father didn't see it that way."

"Your father's a jerk," Lisa said.

"Only on some things," Meg said. "He's really okay. But when he and Mother wouldn't let me talk to you, that made me mad. That's why I came back. To tell you about the gun."

"Where is it now?"

"In the lake. They told me to drop it in the deepest part of the lake." Meg clutched Lisa's hand. "I'm sorry, Lisa, I'm so ashamed to have him for a brother. He didn't mean to hit you, he says he didn't even know you were on the boat. He says he imagined the boat was a big deer and he just wanted to see if he could hit some metal knob at the front of the boat. That's what he says."

"Do you believe him?"

Meg hung her head miserably. "He couldn't have known it was you, how could he?"

"Did the rifle have a telescope do-hickey on it?"

"Something like that."

"Then he knew it was me. Greg says you can see a bird scratching his behind over in Bayside."

"Maybe the gun shot wrong," Meg said. "Maybe he aimed at what he said but didn't figure that the boat was moving."

"Maybe," Lisa said, not believing it.

Meg hugged her. "I'm sorry, Lisa," she said. Then she said, "Do you have to tell the police?"

"God, I don't know."

"My parents will kill me," Meg said.

When they parted, Meg headed back upstate and Lisa walked back to Ralph's house, seeing in her mind sneaky Brucie as the sniper—yes, he would do that—and trying to picture him as the killer of her grandfather and father. That was harder to believe. Certainly he was a wild one when he was on drugs, totally out of his skull, capable of anything. But even wild ones had to have a reason, screwy or not. What was the reason?

A year ago he stole drugs from Gramps's office. But when Gramps was killed, no drugs were missing. If it was Brucie, why didn't he take the drugs? And what reason would Brucie have to kill her father? To get back at her for snubbing him? Not likely. To carry his father's campaign against Marcus Honeywell to the ultimate extreme? But Brucie had no use for his father and wouldn't be likely to take up his cause.

And what was the connection, if any, to California? Only that Brucie had attended the university at Berkeley for a year. That was no damn connection at all!

Arriving at the Simmons house, she told Meg's story to Ralph and Lillian.

Lillian was incensed. "I've a good mind to go over there and shake some decency in him," she said, clenching her fists. "That young man should be sent to reform school. He should be locked up, and they should throw away the key. And that father of his, the pious old fraud, allowing him to buy rifles and drugs and all that, and not knowing what his son was up to, what kind of a parent is that? Ugh!" Her face had gotten alarmingly red.

Ralph said, "Take it easy, Lil. I'm sure Webster is getting his punishment." To Lisa, he said, "I don't know your friend Brucie, but from what you tell me he's probably not the killer. But he *is* the sniper, and I think we ought to tell that to the police so they won't waste any more time looking for him. Not only that, I have a repair bill I'd like to present to Brucie's father."

"What about Meg?" Lisa asked miserably.

Ralph nodded slowly, then went upstairs to his office-at-home. He sat at his desk, took a plain piece of bond paper, and printed in block letters:

TO LIEUTENANT CARBINE—
THE JERK WHO SHOT AT MR. SIMMONS
  BOAT WAS BRUCE WEBSTER.
HE HAD A RIFLE BUT I THINK HE GOT
  RID OF IT.
IM A FRIEND OF HIS AND I DONT WANT
  HIM ARRESTED, JUST SCARE HIM. HE
  NEEDS IT, O.K.?
SCARE HIM GOOD.
    A FRIEND

Lisa stood over him while he printed. He looked up at her. "That ought to do the trick," he said.

She said, "Read it to Aunt Lillian."

He did. Smiling.

Lillian shook her head. "Honestly, Ralph," she said. "Sometimes I think you're in your second childhood."

His smile broadened to a grin.

The next morning Lisa met Eddie Epstein at the Chase Bank in Little Neck. With him were two men, a slickly groomed, jolly man in a three-piece suit who was the branch manager, and a round, expressionless man in a rumpled suit who was the tax department representative.

The bank manager ceremoniously assisted in retrieving the box from the vault and led them to a booth. He deposited the box on the table, said something quietly jolly, smiled, bowed, and backed out. There was only room for the three of them in the booth.

The tax man presided. He sat in one of the chairs, Epstein in the other. Lisa stood behind them. The tax man named aloud each article as he took it from the box. The documents included the deed to her grandfather's house, several insurance policies, a bond and mortgage long since paid off, marriage certificate, Marcus's birth certificate, various diplomas and citations, and an envelope addressed to Marcus containing a number of handwritten pages.

The surprising thing to Lisa was the jewelry, which apparently had belonged to the grandmother she had never known. Gramp's wife had died when Lisa was two. She wasn't even sure what the grandmother had died of. She felt a twinge of guilt that she had never in her life given thought to the woman who had given birth to her father. She must have been a remarkable woman, Lisa thought, to have married the eccentric young veterinarian who would become known as the "Angel of Mercy." There was nothing unusual about the jewelry—diamond engagement ring, wedding band, brooches, earrings, necklaces, pendants, and the like—but Lisa had not expected to see such artifacts of her grandfather's life before a self-centered granddaughter came into it. Her mind wandered . . .

The tax man completed his list, Epstein placed everything from the box in his briefcase and promised to send appraisals of the jewelry to the tax man. They gabbed a few minutes more, small talk about the weather and the man's arthritis. Then the tax man left.

Epstein stood up, peered at Lisa, and said, "Pretty dull stuff."

She said, "What was in that envelope to my father?"

He shrugged and sat down. "Might as well take a look, as long as you're here."

Lisa sat in the other chair. He unfolded the pages from the envelope and started to hand them to her. Then he said, "Why don't I read it out loud for the both of us."

He began reading.

Fifteen

Dear Marc,

You see, you're only two days old and I've already shortened your name from Marcus to Marc! Welcome to the world, you red-faced imp, I hope you find something rewarding to do with your life, something more than just creature comfort, which seems to be the aspiration of most people.

Sorry to sound like a pompous jackass, I forget that when you read this—if you ever read it—you'll probably be a grown man, and the course of your life will be set, for better or worse. I say *if* you read it, because if all seems to be going well with you I may decide to destroy it rather than disturb your peace of mind unnecessarily.

I have a guilt, Marc, and rather than face up to it myself I've passed it on to you, visiting the sin of the father on the child, as they say. I hope I haven't played you a rotten trick.

When you are twenty-one, you will come into some money, a considerable amount of money which I hope will take care of your creature comforts and leave you free to indulge in higher aspirations. A question might arise, however, as to the source of the money. I don't believe it will, but it might.

God, I've written a lot and haven't said a thing. I'm a windy old shitepoke, and that's a fact. Here goes.

It was back in '31, my folks had no money and there were no jobs around, so I bummed across the country looking for work. Seemed like everybody else and his brother were doing the same thing. Anyhow, I got to California and started up the Sacramento Valley until finally there was Mount Shasta saying this is the end of the road, feller. There were others traveling up that valley, but I guess I went farther up in the hills than they did, and that's why I got the job on a sheep ranch.

It was owned by a family named Durango, they didn't speak English very well because they were so isolated up there they didn't get much practice. The father seemed very old to me though he was probably only in his forties. The mother had a leg that was broken and never set properly. The teenage son was a quiet kid named Francisco. Another son named Joaquin was off someplace in college, that's why they needed help. This Joaquin must have been a heck of a worker because they had to hire two guys to take his place, me and a guy named San Sebastian. But to put it bluntly, San Sebastian was a lazy no-good bum.

When I started I didn't know anything about sheep, but as I got to know them I liked them very much, and I especially like the big sheepdog who was there, I think it was a mixed breed, but that was one smart dog. In fact, he did most of the herding, as I remember it. The part I liked best was being out in the fields with him under the big sky, walking lopsided part of the time because the hills were pretty steep in places.

I've got to stop being so gabby. All of this isn't important.

Anyway, I stayed there for nine months until the night of the fire. This no-good bum and I were quartered in a so-called bunkhouse separate from the house the family lived in.

The dog woke us up in the middle of the night, and there was the house blazing away. I was in stocking feet and long johns, but there was no time to put on shoes. This bum and I—he was fully dressed as I remember—we ran to the house and tried to get in, we hollered to the Durangos with the idea of waking them up, but by that time they were probably dead, the smoke was terrible.

Anyhow, I went in there, groped around, went up the stairs as far as I could, then a blast of fire knocked me down to the bottom. I crawled around, I don't know what I had in mind. The little room he used as an office was just breaking into flames. I found the little metal box I knew he kept valuables in, and I barely made it out the front door with the fire biting at my tail.

Why did I save the box? I guess because there were valuables in it and you were supposed to save valuables from being burned up. I later figured what it means is, three people died, but they didn't die poor.

I always suspected that the bum set the fire, but I wasn't sure, so I couldn't do anything.

I was unconscious for a minute, and I woke up with the bum trying to take the box from me. Then he said, let's split it. He didn't even know what was in it, but he wanted to grab half if he couldn't get it all. I said, no, it belongs to the kid who's in college. I was strong enough to make that stick.

I won't go into all the details because they're not important. I hid the box to keep him from running off with it.

But there were just the two of us with about a hundred sheep that didn't belong to us, and neither of us able to take care of them for long. Winter was just starting, there was a lot to do, but the bum wouldn't do anything, just sneak around looking for the box. So we had a fight, and I ran him off the property, leaving me and the dog alone with the sheep. Then a wolf got one of the lambs, and I had to do something. I knew that by winter's end they'd all be dead, and the son wouldn't be coming back until spring.

There was a wool dealer down near Redding, I went to him, sold him the sheep, went back to the ranch with the money, and waited until the dealer came and herded the animals away. Meanwhile the wolves got two more lambs. I should have thought to buy a shotgun but I didn't. I did kill one of the wolves with a rock, lucky shot, I was a pretty good baseball pitcher in those days, but that was all luck, believe me.

That left the dog and me alone. We were good friends. His name was Chico, he didn't look like a Chico to me, but, well, never mind. What I planned to do was take the money and the valuables to the nearest bank I could find and leave it there in the name of Joaquin Durango and tell the wool dealer so he could tell Joaquin when he finally returned. I didn't trust the dealer enough to leave it all with him. In fact, I didn't trust him at all, he shouldn't have taken my bill of sale and given me the money, I didn't own the sheep. I just hoped he would be honest enough to tell Joaquin.

So Chico and I started down the road, just a path really, and we came to where it curved through the woods. Like the innocent fool that I was, I was completely surprised by the shotgun blast that came out of nowhere and nearly parted my hair. There was this San Sebastian standing in the path with a shotgun leveled at me. Obviously, he had bought the darn thing and come back.

He called me Buddy in a sarcastic way. He said, "Just lay that box on the ground, old buddy, and start running."

I had a pretty good idea he was going to shoot me in the back, so I edged toward him, me and Chico, and began talking, not saying anything. When we got close he was starting to panic, and I could see he was about to fire. So I said, "Okay, okay, I'm doing it!" and I bent down to put the box there.

Well, Chico had been growling all along, and his hackles were up. Then the bum must have made a move the dog didn't like, and Chico leaped at him. The gun went off and ripped Chico apart, but his momentum knocked San Sebastian backward. I knew the poor dog was a goner, but I also knew the bum had now fired two shells, and what with the dog knocking him off balance, it would take a couple of seconds for the bum to reload. So I took off into the woods like a scared jackrabbit, which is what I was.

The son of a gun was faster than I thought because I was still in sight when he fired again. Two of the pellets actually hit me. I ran like Glenn Cunningham except this was more like the hurdles, not a flat race track.

Well, you don't want to know the rest of it. The fact is, I still had the box with me. For a while I was lost. Knowing that ornery shitepoke like I did, I knew he was going to follow me to the ends of the earth if he could. So I kept on the run all the way back here to Little Neck.

Except for Cheyenne. It was in Cheyenne I decided I was doing the wrong thing and that I ought to go back and leave the money in a bank as I had started out to do. But that blankety-blank bum caught up to me there, and I was lucky to get away from him. I sometimes think God had other plans for me than to be stabbed to death in that old freight yard. I swear He put an iron pipe there where my hand could find it and bash the bum in the head. But it started me running again.

So there you have it, Marcus my lad. That money became your inheritance. A couple of times I put ads in the Redding paper telling the Durango son to get in touch with me, but I never heard anything, and then I stopped doing it. I should have done more, but I didn't. Time goes by, and you forget.

I owed my life to Chico, so I dedicated the rest of my life to him, a mongrel sheepdog. But you don't want to hear all that.

All I want to say now is, dedicate your life to something worthwhile—Be a shepherd of something, not of sheep, but of something other than yourself. It's really a selfish thing to do because it will bring you rewards you wouldn't have otherwise.

Oh, Lord, I'm preaching again.

Have some fun too, darn it.

    With all my love,
    Your Dad

Lisa took the letter with her to her room at the Simmons house, and slowly read it through by herself, her lips moving. Then she read it again. Her emotions were in a jumble.

Weeping, she thought of her father who was once a "red-faced imp," who grew up to dedicate himself—well, sort of—to public service as an assemblyman, who had had some fun, too, in all too short a time. And she thought of her beloved grandfather, and she was painfully proud of both of them.

The next day she went home to her own house on Shore Road.

Sixteen

ALONE IN THE BIG HOUSE, she realized she had moved away from comparative safety into the danger zone: all she could do now was wait for the killer to draw near in the darkness, pick his own sweet time, and pounce. Not entirely alone, of course. The two maids were there in the daytime, but they did nothing but gab all day long, driving Lisa crazy. Her grandfather was the one who called them Brenda and Cobina, apparently thinking the names were funny, but those weren't their real names.

To get away from them, she went back to work at Macy's. Greg was still occupied with his summer job in one of Jack Doran's lawn crews. She had imposed on Ralph and Lillian Simmons long enough. It was time she took charge of her own life. The feeling of being adrift without a destination no longer gave her that queasiness in her stomach. There were even times when she felt her old happy-go-lucky self.

Eddie Epstein said there was no need for her to work at Macy's if she didn't want to.

She said, "What else would I do?"

He said, "Act like other rich kids, buy Guccis and Puccis, go to discos, snort coke, ski in the Austrian Alps instead of Hunter Mountain, buy a villa on the Riviera, get a classier car—"

"I *like* my car," she said indignantly.

He shook his head sadly. "You'll never make it as a rich girl," he said. "You don't even want to be one of the Beautiful People."

"I look all right," she said.

Epstein kept her busy with various matters relating to the two estates.

Ralph Simmons dropped by most evenings to tell her the latest joke he had heard or bring her some rich concoction from Lillian's kitchen. He made her feel good.

So did Paulie Doran, of all people, just by following her in the security patrol car. So did the real NYPD prowl cars that frequently lingered in front of the house while on their rounds.

Greg came in the evenings and stayed with her. He displayed a new sensitivity by not trying to get her upstairs and into bed at every opportunity, realizing, glory be, that the time was not right, that what Lisa needed most of all was a soothing presence, simply that, while she got used to being alone in the world.

Uncle Shaky, too, took her mind off her own problems. She thought of having him move into the big house with her but wisely decided against it. Her nerves weren't up to having a sick person so near.

Lieutenant Joseph Carbine came one evening to tell her about the anonymous note he had received. He said he had given Bruce Webster a really good scare. "That's what you wanted, wasn't it?" he said.

She said, "What do you mean?"

He said, "I guess it doesn't matter, so long as the young man has learned his lesson. Do you think he'll come after you again? He could be a dangerous young man."

She said, "I can handle Brucie."

The first attack came from an unexpected source. It came on the second night she was back at work. That day she was on the late shift, and she arrived home at nine-forty-five after helping to close the store. She parked in the driveway, and as she walked across the lawn to the front of the house she was intercepted by a hunched-over man with a pale, bloated face. Startled, she touched the handcuffs in her back pocket for reassurance.

"Just a minute, Miss Honeywell," the man said. His voice was not friendly.

She recognized him as Charles Raymond, the husband of her father's murdered secretary. She remembered vaguely that he had originally come from the West Coast, which was interesting, but—

"We have a few things to talk about," he said. "Let's go in the house."

"No." She moved off the grass onto the path. "It's a nice night. We can talk here if you want."

The man made a sound in his throat. "You're a snooty bitch, just like your father. I'm not good enough to enter your house."

She looked down at the empty roadway and thought, Where the hell are all my damn guardians when I need them? She wondered if she was strong enough to use the handcuffs if the man gave her trouble.

She said, "That's impolite, Mr. Raymond. Good night." She turned toward the steps to the front door.

He grabbed her arm. "Don't pull that princess act on me, young woman," he growled. "Your father was a murderer, and he owes restitution. That what I want—restitution."

He was hurting her arm. She told him to let go. Her free hand had the handcuffs out of her pocket behind her. Too bad she wasn't licensed for a gun, she thought. All she had were the cuffs.

His dark eyes were fixed on her. "Blood money," he said. "Blood money is bad luck money unless you make restitution. It's the only way. Restitution!"

She tried to pull away, but his grip only tightened, He was pulling her toward him. She smelled the booze on his breath and knew she was dealing with an irrational person.

In panic, she lashed him across the face with the handcuffs, forcing him to stagger back. Figuring that if she ran up the steps he would be on her before she could open the door, she faced him in a crouch, the cuffs dangling in one hand. She debated whether to scream in the hope that someone would come running. But Lisa Honeywell had never screamed in her life, not even at horror movies. It was a matter of pride: she refused to be the weak sister that boys expected girls to be. *The hell with you, you shitepoke, I can take care of myself* had always been her attitude. Now she insisted to herself, I can handle this crazy wino, I can handle him—

"Go home, Mr. Raymond," she said. "That's blood on your cheek. You want more, I'll give it to you on the other side. Come on, Mr. Raymond, let's see how a big strong man beats up on a girl—"

Her last words seemed to infuriate him. He leaped at her, clutched the wrist of her hand holding the cuffs, and walloped the side of her head with his free hand, stunning her. Tears blurred her vision.

"I'll teach you respect, girlie," he said hoarsely.

She rammed her head into his belly, heard him grunt. She felt him pounding on her back, then suddenly—he wasn't there. Somebody was holding him, pinning his arms to his side. She straightened up and gaped.

"Hey, old bull," a voice said. "It ain't a sportin' thing to manhandle a little lady like that. Ah think you oughta be ashamed of yourself, sir. Are you all right, Miss Honeywell?"

For a moment she was speechless, astonished to see that her rescuer was not one of her self-appointed guardians but the paradigm of Texas gallantry, Jack Doran. She had always been suspicious of his effusive good will, figuring it was all a charming put-on to drum up business. The gold buttons on the sleeve of his blazer glittered in the shadow.

"No sweat, Mr. Doran," she said as sweetly as she could. Her ear was still ringing from the clout she had received. "But it's good you came along. Watch out for your shoes, it looks like the big brave man is about to throw up."

Doran threw the man down on the lawn. "He's that woman's husband, isn't he? What's his name again?"

"Raymond. I think it's Charles Raymond."

Doran nudged the man with his foot. "Listen, Charlie, if you throw up on that nice lawn, you're gonna clean it up, y'hear?"

He said to Lisa, "Go call the police. This fella's not goin' anywhere."

She hesitated. "He called my father's money *blood* money. I want to know why he called it that. He acted as if it was his money. It doesn't make sense."

Doran nudged the man again. "Answer the little lady, Charlie. Why'd you call it blood money?"

The man on the lawn glared up at Lisa. "I told her. Because her father was a bloody murderer, that's why."

Doran kicked him in the ribs. "That wasn't a nice thing to say, Charlie." Doran looked at Lisa. "Anything else you want to know?"

"Yes. Where in California did he come from? And does he have any relatives still living out there?"

Doran nudged the man. "Where in California. Charlie?"

The man gaped at Lisa. "This kid is crazy," he said. "Lemme outa here." He struggled to rise, and Doran held him down with his foot.

"Where, Charlie?"

"Pasadena. But what the hell difference—?"

"Do you have any relatives out there?"

"How the hell do I know? I haven't seen them for twenty years!"

Doran looked questioningly at Lisa.

She said, "Was one of his relatives named San Sebastian?"

Doran moved his foot, but the man stopped him by saying quickly, "You don't have to do that, damn it! No, I don't know that name!"

Doran said to Lisa, "The hombre claims he doesn't know the name."

It struck Lisa that Gentleman Jack Doran was enjoying the game. She shook her head and grinned. "Let the hombre go, Mr. Doran. I'll tell the police that he tried to beat me up, but he was too weak. They'll keep an eye on him."

Doran said, "Would you like to give him one last kick in the ribs, ma'am? It'll make you feel good."

Lisa laughed and declined the invitation. Doran's deadpan role playing was very funny.

As they watched the man scamper away, she thanked her rescuer. "Mah pleasure, ma'am," he said, his accent becoming even more exaggerated. "Ah couldn't let anyone damage this here im-maculate lawn, now could Ah?"

She invited him into the house for a drink, but he said the hour was late.

He said in a more serious tone, "A sweet girl like you shouldn't be all alone in a big house like this. There are some mighty peculiar critters roamin' this earth, and they have no milk of human kindness in them. Varmints who eat up little girls like you."

"I can take care of myself," she said in automatic response.

He said, "You were doin' fine, ma'am, just fine against that wretch of a man, but he's not the kind of varmint Ah'm talkin' about."

She peered back at her house, frowning. "Well, I've been thinking of putting in an alarm system. I guess I ought to do that."

"Good idea," he said. "And if you'll permit me, I know just the man to install it. Guaranteed burglar-proof. And I might add, killer-proof. Forgive me for mentioning it, but Ah've noticed some killin's goin' on around here. You plant yourself in that big house of yours—we'll make a fortress out of it—and no one's gonna get at you. No one!"

"Well, okay then, do that," she said. Impulsively she gave him a kiss on his cheek.

"Ah," he said, sighing. "Lisa kissed me. Like in that poem, how does it go? 'Say Ah'm weary, say Ah'm sad, something, something, but add, Jenny kissed me!' You've made mah day, Miss Lisa!"

She had never heard of the poem, but she laughed along with Jack Doran.

He mounted the steps with her, saw that she was safely inside her door. He bowed and started away. At the foot of the steps, he turned and said, "Meanwhile, if any varmint tries to bother you, just holler. Ah'm generally round about, and if you holler loud enough, chances are Ah'll hear you."

They both laughed again. He got in his car, which he had parked down on the road, and drove off. She hugged herself, thinking, So I've got another guardian I didn't know about.

But in the cool center hall of the house, the feeling of well-being drained away, and she felt terribly alone.

The next morning, a reluctance to talk to the police and the fact that she had to hurry to get to the store on time kept her from reporting the incident to Lieutenant Carbine. In the evening when both Ralph Simmons and Greg Muldavin were there, she told them what had happened.

"Why didn't you kick him, sweetie pie?" Greg said. "If it was me, I'd have kicked him—just one kick—with these"—he pointed to his work shoes— "I'd have broken five ribs!" He laughed idiotically.

Ralph Simmons said, "You don't think he's the California connection?"

"Can't be," she said. "He came from California, that's all. But his brains are mush. Can you picture him doing—what the killer did?" Sudden flashes of memory put a catch in her voice.

"Hard to picture anyone doing it," Ralph said.

"He was crazy mad. You should have seen him."

Greg said to Ralph, "I offered her a gun, and the knucklehead wouldn't take it. Don't you think she should have a gun to protect herself, Mr. Simmons?"

"Hard to say, Greg," Ralph replied mildly. "I don't think she should be here alone, that's what I think." He looked questioningly at Lisa.

"No," she said firmly. "Once I get the burglar alarms in, nobody'll have to worry about me. It's my house, and no damn shitepoke's gonna scare me out of it!"

"How about the knife then?" Greg said.

Lisa sighed. "Oh, Gregory."

Ralph said, "We should tell Carbine about this."

"Go ahead," she said. "Maybe he can put a scare in him like he did to Brucie."

The next day when she came home from work, the alarm man was just finishing installation of the system. Jack Doran was with him. The man showed her how it worked. "You just have to remember to turn it on with this switch." He pointed to a small box affixed out of sight to the underside of the hall table. "And if you come in the door when the alarm is on, you have twenty seconds to switch it off if you don't want to blast the eardrums of your neighbors."

"It'll blast more eardrums than that!" Doran exclaimed. "Listen to this baby!" He tripped the alarm, and the sirenlike wail was a screech out of hell.

"That'll shatter eardrums of folks across the bay! Ain't that a lollapalooza!"

Slowly Lisa began to feel safe and snug in her home, the way it had been when her father was alive. The maids took care of the household chores, including buying her food at the Savage Point Market. She suspected a little of the money was slipping into their own purses, but what the hell, she thought, it was just like giving them a raise in pay, so no problem.

Greg was acting more maturely these days, and she felt safest when she was in his arms. One evening, after returning from a movie in Bayside, they brought Mallomars and hot coffee to her room, and leaning against the headboard of her bed they watched a rerun of "Kojak."

Greg was unusually subdued, and during a commercial he said softly, "Do you know what I want most in this world?"

"What?"

He sighed. "I act like a jackass sometimes, I know that. And you deserve someone better than me. No, no, you're so damn beautiful, sweetie, I keep wondering why you stay with me. I keep being afraid some good-looking son of a bitch is gonna come along and grab you . . . What I would like is to be better looking and smarter and richer like—well, like Magnum, Tom Selleck, so I wouldn't lose you—"

"Magnum's not rich," she said.

"No, but Selleck is," Greg said. "And that's what's gonna happen, you know it and I know it, and when that rich guy comes along I'm gonna kill him, but only in my head because I wouldn't do a thing like that to you if you really wanted the son of a bitch—"

She put her hand over his mouth to stop the flow of words.

"Okay, Thomas Magnum, what are you going to do now?" she said.

He turned toward her and proceeded to show her what the handsome Hawaiian PI would do. "Kojak" ended, but they weren't aware of it.

He spent the entire night with her for the first time in their lives.

Lisa felt that everything was right with the world once again.

She became careless as the summer ran down into fall.

Seventeen

THE FIRST ONE to trip the alarm was the mailman. The only occupants at the time were the maids, who went into a fluttering tizzy and couldn't work for the rest of the day. Ralph Simmons heard it many blocks away and came speeding to the scene. He discovered that the alarm man had engaged in a bit of overkill: he had placed a sensor in the mail slot!

"Dumbest thing I ever saw," he told Lisa that evening. "What did that guy think would happen? Somebody would shoot poison gas through the slot? Or maybe the world's smallest midget would climb through and stab you in the toe! Unbelievable!"

Until the alarm circuit could be rectified, Lisa hung a basket for the mail outside the door.

Another time it was Greg Muldavin who set it off. He was back at school, which was only a few miles away from Savage Point. One night he sneaked away from his dorm to visit Lisa. Thinking it would be fun to surprise her, he climbed through a sunroom window. Unfortunately, he had forgotten about the alarm system. The police came with guns drawn, and he had an embarrassing few minutes of explanation.

After that, Lisa's liking for the system waned, and at times when her mind was preoccupied she would neglect to flick it on, or conversely, forget to switch it off within the twenty-second grace period when entering the house.

The police became sluggish in responding, a development that nearly cost Lisa her life.

One raw October night when she was on the late shift at Macy's, she didn't arrive home until ten-fifteen. She was surprised to see that Bruce Webster was waiting for her, slouched on the front steps. He peered up at her with bleared eyes.

"Brucie," she exclaimed, "I thought you were away at college. What are you doing here?"

"My dear, sweet father kicked me outa the house," he said, slurring his words.

"But what about college? It was another one in California, wasn't it?"

"Kicked out," he said, blinking. "Everywhere I go, kicked out. Story of my life."

A twinge of pity edged its way through the feeling of contempt in Lisa. "Gee, that's tough, Brucie. But you can't stay here, it wouldn't look right." Lisa didn't really care how it "looked" to neighbors, she just didn't want Bruce Webster in her house. Carbine had called him dangerous, and though at the moment he appeared to be pretty well zonked out on downers she was afraid he would quickly return to his normal nasty self.

A chill wind was coming off the bay, and he shivered.

"That's okay, I'll find somewhere," he said. "Only wanted to ask you something. It's been on my mind

... Hey, who turned on the air conditioning?" He hugged his arms, and she noticed he was wearing a short-sleeved summer shirt.

With a sigh of exasperation, she said, "Come on in, and I'll make you some coffee."

"You don't have to do that," he said.

"No problem," she said.

He followed her into the house and stood swaying in the hall while she reached under the table and switched off the alarm. She led him to the kitchen and sat him at the table; then she put a pot of water on the stove to heat. When she turned her gaze back to him, she was shocked to see that he was much more alert, and there was a frightening gleam in his eyes, red for danger.

She started to say, "Now what was it you wanted to ask—"

"Where's your lover boy tonight?"

She glanced at the kitchen clock and said as casually as she could, "You mean Greg? He'll be here any minute now."

Bruce slowly stood up. Having known him since childhood, she hadn't been so acutely aware of how big and bulky he had become.

He loomed over her, grinning slyly. "You just made that up, didn't you? He's not really coming, is he?"

She put a hand on his chest. "If you're getting ideas, forget them, Brucie," she said, remembering the last time he had tried to manhandle her: she had slammed her knee into his crotch, then others had intervened. Now there were no others to intervene.

She said, "Do you want coffee or don't you?"

His body pressed forward against her hand, and for a moment she thought he was actually going to attack her. The Honeywell carving knives were three steps away, but the thought of using one repelled her. She increased the pressure against his chest.

"Sit down!" she ordered him.

A look of uncertainty crossed his face, and he cried, "Okay! Okay!" He plunked in a chair and glared at her. "Just trying to be friendly, that's all," he said.

"You have some idea of friendly," she said.

"So do you," he shot back.

She moved away from him and rested her buttocks against a counter. "What did you want to ask me?" she said sweetly.

His eyes lost focus as he tried to line up his thoughts, then they took on a knowing look. "It was you who told the cops, wasn't it? I suppose you think that was a friendly thing to do, to stab me in the back like that. You've always hated me, haven't you?"

She sensed a wild passion starting to build up in him, and she said, "I'm trying to be friendly, Brucie. Do you want cream and sugar? You can use the phone if you want to. One of your friends will probably let you in."

Abruptly his face screwed up, and he was crying. "They won't! I tried! Their damn fathers are against me! Everybody's against me, and it's all your fault! You started it!"

"Oh, for God's sake, Brucie," she said. The knives were within reach, but she shrank from touching them.

His face composed itself into a look of angry grievance. "You sent that damned note to the cops, didn't you? Meg told you about the gun, and you told the cops. Don't lie! You turned my sister against me and my father against me, and you put the cops on me! How friendly can you get? And let me ask you this—what did you do in Los Angeles? The fucking college was against me right from the start, and then they kicked me out for no reason at all! What friendly thing did you say to them, Lisa? Did you give them money?"

"Just listen to yourself," she said. "You're talking crazy. Come on now, have some coffee and straighten up."

She turned off the burner under the water. With her back still turned to him, she said, "Talking about friendly, it wasn't exactly friendly when you shot at me and sent glass all over me. But let's forget—"

Suddenly she was being embraced from the rear, and rough hands were clutching her breasts. In the first moment of shock, she froze. Brucie was saying in her ear, "You been sleeping around, baby. Everybody knows that. Now it's my turn."

He abruptly tugged her away from the stove, and she noted with interest that her hands were holding the pot of boiling water. Some of it spilled as he tried to wrestle her to the floor.

"Brucie!" She stamped her heel down on his instep.

He grunted in pain and for a moment stopped his violent motions.

"That was just to get your attention, damn it," she said. "Notice what I have in my hands. Water, you stupid shitepoke. A minute ago it was boiling. So the question is, do you want me to dump it on your head, I can do it, you know."

Bruce stood still, and she imagined his eyes staring at the water. "You're nuts," he said. "It'd go all over you, not me."

"Do you wanna take the chance? Come on, you have nothing to lose but your face."

His hands slowly came away from her ripping the fabric of her blouse as they did so. Suddenly he was lunging around her, grabbing at the pot handle. Expecting the move, she half turned and sloshed the water backward toward him, scalding his left arm. Some of it spattered on her own arm and side.

He screamed and called her a short litany of foul names. "You tried to kill me!" he gasped.

Lisa, despite the shock of the burning water, scrambled toward the door to the hall. Behind her, Bruce was crying wildly, telling the mute walls and white appliances, "She tried to kill me! Did you see that? She tried to skin me alive!"

In the hall she raced to the phone on the hall table, saying to herself, 911 . . . 911. She succeeded in dialing the number, and a voice was answering when Bruce lumbered into the hall after her, looking like all the scary things in horror movies put together.

She dropped the phone, reached under the table, and fumbled for the switch to turn on the alarm system. *The front door,* she thought; *gotta open it, slam into it—*

He caught her before she could touch it. His arm came down like a club and walloped her on the side of her head, knocking her to the floor. Her hand reached out and accidentally—miraculously—hit the mail slot. She had intended to have the sensor removed but had never gotten around to it. The sudden screeching wail was the most beautiful sound she had ever heard!

But Bruce Webster didn't hear it. He was on her, slugging her, ripping her clothes, tugging at the tight jeans which refused to slide off. She focused her energy on warding off the blows, wondering where the hell were the damn police. She tried to roll away, but the weight of his body prevented it. When he used both hands to unbuckle her belt, she flailed at his face; she raised her head and butted him in the nose. From below it looked like a pig's snout. Blood from the nose splattered her face. He punched the side of her jaw, making her senses reel.

Where were the damn police?

He had the jeans unzipped and bunched at her knees. Her fingernails dug into his face. He tore her panties off. She kept her legs tightly together. He walloped her face again, and she blacked out for a moment. The jeans were at her ankles. His knee was spreading her legs, his hands were clawing at her.

She had once heard that it was nearly impossible to rape an unwilling woman, something about a thread and the eye of a needle. *Right on*, she thought grimly; *this damn shitepoke's not gonna get in me. I'll kill him first, I'll kill him.* He was fumbling with his own clothes. She punched him in the stomach, and in retaliation he slammed his fist into her face. The lights faded . . .

She continued to squirm and strike out, muttering, "No you don't, you fucking shit!"

She was hitting air.

A hand touched her forehead, and she swiveled her head away.

A voice said, "Easy does it, Lisa." She swung a fist, and a hand caught it. "Whoa! Just lie still a moment. You're okay." Her struggling subsided.

She looked up into the blurry face of Ralph Simmons.

He said, "Just lie still a moment. Looks like you've had another concussion. Is anything broken?"

She said, "Where—where—?"

"Brucie? I persuaded him to cease and desist by the judicious application of a poker from your fireplace. I think I broke his skull."

She became aware of the body on the floor beside her. She also became aware that she was quite naked except for the jeans at her ankles. She said, "I think maybe I ought to get something on me." She sat up and tugged at her jeans.

Ralph took off his shirt and gave it to her. "Any dizziness?" he asked.

"No."

He said, "From the look of him, slugger, you were ahead on points when I stopped the bout."

"Is he dead?" she asked.

"Do you care?"

She thought a moment. "No. . . . Yes! . . . I don't know." It was hard to think with the alarm still screeching outside.

Ralph didn't turn it off until the police arrived.

Two hours later they were sitting with Lillian in the Simmons parlor, sipping hot chocolate, feeling depressed by the news that Bruce Webster did indeed have a fractured skull and was in intensive care at North Shore Hospital.

Lisa said, "I think he would have killed me. Not on purpose, but that's what would have happened. He was crazy."

Ralph said, "I agree. With all those drugs in him, I don't think he would have been able to succeed in raping you. That would have enraged him still further, and there's no telling what he would have done."

Lillian Simmons was in a state of outrage. "Slime!" she muttered.

Ralph said, "We were watching "The Equalizer" when I heard the alarm. The Equalizer was going into the empty warehouse after the gang of sadistic murderers. How did it turn out, Lil?"

"How do you think it turned out?" she said. "That they killed him and went on their evil way? Have you ever noticed, Lisa, what lousy shots the bad guys are on television? The worst thing that ever happens to the hero is he gets cracked on the head from behind, but does he ever get a fractured skull? Never! Do any of the bullets ever hit him? Never!"

"Why do you keep watching?" Lisa asked.

Lillian grinned. "Because they're fun."

A minute later, Ralph said. "So Brucie was in California. I can't imagine him strangling San Sebastian, can you?"

Lisa shook her head somberly. "With a crazy person, anything is possible," she said. "The whole thing doesn't make sense. He stole drugs from Gramps's office, I'm pretty sure of that. But there's no way he could have killed him, I don't think. Or my father. Or Mrs. Raymond. It doesn't make sense."

Lillian Simmons scowled. "He tried to kill you on the boat! I'll always believe he was aiming at you and not some dumb knob up front."

Ralph sighed. "As Lisa said, with a crazy person anything is possible. Thank God this particular one will be out of circulation for a long, long while."

Eighteen

SHE STAYED AT the Simmons's house three more days. The left side of her face was swollen, and it seemed that every muscle and joint in her body ached. The concussion was a mild one, but the doctor considered it serious, coming as it did on top of the severe one she had gotten in the plane crash.

"Lucky it was my head," she said to Ralph. "There's nothing in it that can hurt."

Ralph said, "Don't sell yourself short, honey. You have more smarts than a lot of people I know. There was a guy in the Army with me who had an IQ in the genius class and he could never strip and clean his rifle. They made him a clerk, and he wasn't very good at that either. Arnold Something. Wonder what ever happened to him."

On the second day she became restless. She took walks with Ralph, holding her head as motionless as she could. "You don't have to do that," Ralph said. "There's no case on record of a head falling off during an easy walk. At least not in Savage Point."

The leaves were changing color, and there was a fall nip in the air. By the end of the day she felt almost normal. At North Shore Hospital Bruce Webster was taken off the critical list, though he still remained in intensive care.

At ten-thirty in the gray morning of the third day, a convocation of sorts took place in the Simmons's living room. It was instigated by Bruce's parents, Malcolm and Eunice Webster. They arrived first, but seeing no other cars in the driveway remained in their sedate Buick sedan by the side of the street. A fine drizzle hung in the air, and they kept their windshield wipers working.

Ralph Simmons, peering through the window at the unmoving couple in the parked car, said, "I don't know why that's a funny sight, but it is."

"They look like store dummies, that's why," Lisa said.

Eddie Epstein and Lieutenant Joseph Carbine arrived within seconds of each other, and they all entered the house led by the now militant figure of Malcolm Webster, who was complaining about lateness.

They seated themselves in the small living room, bringing with them the dusty, damp smell of the drizzle. Ralph and Lillian brought out coffee and cups along with sugar and cream, and went through the serving ceremonies. Eunice rattled her cup in her saucer and with a mortified look placed it carefully on the coffee table and would never again touch it.

Lieutenant Carbine spoke first. "I have no official standing here," he said. "The matter of Bruce Webster is in the hands of the Queens district attorney. We supply the evidence, and they take it from there. I'm here because Mr. Webster asked me to be here."

He looked at Ralph. "Incidentally, Mr. Simmons, the matter of your attack on young Mr. Webster, no matter how justified it seems, has to be presented to the grand jury, but I'm told there's no way they'll indict you."

Ralph felt the eyes of the parents on him and held back the flip reply that was on his lips. He said, "I'm relieved, Lieutenant. I wish there had been some other way to subdue the young man, but I'm not as strong as I used to be. It was a question of his life or Lisa's."

"Oh come on, Mr. Simmons," Malcolm Webster interjected. "I admit that Bruce was not himself, but I'm sure that Miss Honeywell's *life* was never in danger."

Ralph said quietly, "I didn't want to wait to find out."

Eddie Epstein rapped the coffee table. "Let's not get off on the wrong foot. We're here to discuss a proposal from Mr. Webster, not who should have done what to whom. You have the floor, Mr. Webster."

Webster was leaning forward in his chair with his forearms on his knees. Lisa thought he looked like a giant frog in a three-piece suit.

"Yes," Webster said, clearing his throat. "It's simply this. Our Bruce somehow has gone down the wrong road. We tried to be good parents and give him guidance, but we never realized the strength of peer pressure. He got in with a group of boys—"

Carbine interrupted. "Bruce is twenty-two years old, sir."

"I'm talking about when he was a teenager, Lieutenant," Webster went on smoothly. "His so-called friends introduced him to drugs, starting with marijuana and wine, a lethal enough combination in itself, but they led him on from there into cocaine and into drugs I don't even know the names of. Thank God they never got into heroin.

"The point is our Bruce became an addict. There's no other word for it, he was, and is, an addict. Eunice and I should have caught on to this a long time ago, but the fact is, we didn't. That's our fault."

Eunice Webster whimpered and put a tissue to her nose. He clasped her other hand.

Lisa, watching, was moved. It was like watching a soap opera.

Eddie Epstein said, "You're telling us something we know, Mr. Webster. He's an addict, and we feel sorry for you. But this addict of yours sent a bullet within an inch of Lisa's head with a rifle with a telescopic lens—"

"Prove that!" Webster said, raising his voice.

"Then he entered her home," Epstein went on, "and he attacked her, tried to rape her, and came within an ace of killing her."

"Wrong!" Webster shouted. "Wrong! If Bruce tried to attack her sexually, I'm sure he had some provocation, and he certainly was *not* within an ace of killing her, as you say!"

"Provocation!" Lisa cried. "Are you saying—?"

Ralph held up a hand to halt her. "Let me handle this, honey." He stood up and turned to Webster. "I think you owe Lisa an apology. If you don't do it right now, this meeting is over and you're marching the hell out of here."

The policeman Carbine glanced from one to the other of the two men with a look of amused interest on his face.

Webster looked startled. "I—I didn't mean to say that," he stammered. "I was only thinking of Bruce and what was going through his drugged mind. I did not wish to imply any misconduct on your part, Miss Honeywell."

"You're the one who kicked him out of the house," she said, "without a coat. I let him in because he was freezing."

Webster let a moment slip by, and then said smoothly, "Be that as it may. We're here to do something positive to help our son. For the sake of argument, I concede that we were at fault in handling Brucie and that he committed a criminal act in attacking Miss Honeywell. But he is not basically a criminal. He would never dream of injuring Miss Honeywell or breaking the law in any way—"

"Like breaking into my grandfather's office and stealing drugs?" Lisa said. "Did he tell you about that?"

Webster's clasped hands tightened, but he held his temper. "What I'm trying to say, Miss Honeywell, is that whatever he did, it wasn't the real Bruce Webster who did them, it was the coke or the crack or the whatever that was doing them. I know it's late in the game, but we're convinced that if we cure him of the habit, he'll be the straight and upright citizen he would have been if left alone. Now, there's an organization in Suffolk County that's one of the best detoxification centers in the country. Their success ratio is eighty percent. They specialize in young people."

He sighed deeply and went on. "What we wish to propose to the district attorney—but we wanted to talk it over with you people first, because if Miss Honeywell insists on pressing charges the district attorney may find it difficult to go along with our proposal—what we want to do is commit our son to this detoxification center and get him properly straightened out."

He peered somberly at Lisa. "The district attorney's choice depends to a large extent on what you choose to do, Lisa." He tried to smile warmly in using her first name, as if to establish a joining of intentions between the two of them. "If you feel vindictive toward our Brucie, then you will very likely be sending him to prison for a number of years. Let me say this, prison would ruin him. He would be beyond redemption. But at this moment in his life he can still be saved. It's up to you, Lisa."

In the silence that followed, he continued to stare at her.

Lisa felt confused and resentful. This imposing man was attempting to put a tremendous burden on her, making her judge and jury in the fate of his worthless son. She felt she was being put on trial instead of the man who attacked her.

She started to say, "It's not up to me—"

Eddie Epstein interrupted. "Seems to me," he said, "the best detoxification program is a couple of years in prison without drugs, don't you agree?"

Webster answered him. Epstein talked again, then Ralph Simmons spoke. One of the things Ralph said was, "We have to be absolutely sure that this young man will never again be free to have another go at Miss Honeywell."

The voices rumbled on, with Lisa only half listening. Eddie Epstein and Ralph Simmons were rejecting Webster's proposal. Even Lillian Simmons had her say, and it made sense to Lisa.

"The way I understand it," Lillian said, "the person we're talking about has more than a drug problem. He's all mixed up about sex. They say such a person is dangerous, because he's a man and yet not a man, if you know what I mean. To me he's a slimy young squirt—"

Eunice Webster stiffened, and Malcolm Webster said, "Now see here—"

"But the important thing is not what I think," Lillian went on. "It's what he thinks of himself. All he has to do is look in the mirror, for crying out loud. He has to know he's a slob and no woman in her right mind would let him touch her. All I know about young men is they want to you-know-what with the girls. And if they can't do it, then sooner or later they're gonna explode and wind up killing somebody. That's the part of him that has to be fixed as much as the drug part."

"Oh, he'll have counseling on that score too," Webster said. "Don't you worry—"

"Counseling schmounseling," Lillian said. "If it was up to me, I'd get him a nice motherly prostitute—"

Epstein and Ralph burst out laughing.

"Find one for me, too," Epstein said.

Finally they all looked at Lisa. A word Malcolm Webster had used stuck in her mind. *Vindictive.* In her mind it meant more than *an eye for an eye,* it meant blind hatred, a curse calling down all the ills of heaven and earth on the hated object, and—in its most virulent form—a vendetta against the victim aimed at obliterating him and his whole line of progeny.

She said, "I am not vindictive, I'm not! That's a form of crazy. I just want Brucie to stay away from me. I don't care how it's done, just keep him away, okay?"

Then she surprised herself by starting to cry.

Nineteen

THE LONELINESS STOLE in on her slowly like the chill of the winter that was still two months away. She filled her days with enough activity to keep the chill at bay. She threw herself into her detective work at Macy's and almost single-handedly reduced the pilferage to a trickle, at the same time incurring the enmity not only of professional shoplifters but of larcenous sales clerks as well. One clerk—from Sports—waylaid her in the parking lot and stomped her several times before she was able to hook his leg with hers and topple him to the pavement. She had sore ribs for a week.

She had to take time off to testify before the grand jury regarding the assault by Bruce Webster and also against two shoplifters at a court in Mineola. Bruce was indicted, but his trial was put off while Malcolm Webster and two hired psychiatrists worked on the district attorney, who belonged to the same political party as Webster. When Bruce was released from the hospital, he was remanded to the custody of the detoxification tank in Suffolk County.

She was alone in the big house on Shore Road. Her isolation was brought home to her when the last pleasure boat was gone from the bay, and the empty slate-gray water reflected the autumnal sky. She spent more time at the Savage Point Club vainly seeking a common bond with the regulars who drank too much.

On her twenty-first birthday, she grimly experimented with alcohol to determine her capacity. The next night when the Simmonses took her out to dinner to celebrate, she reported the result.

"Five Seven-and-Sevens in two and a half hours is too much. I got dizzy. So it must be four. I didn't feel anything else except I wanted to punch somebody in the mouth."

"Is that the only thing you drink?" Ralph asked.

"The Seven-Up kills the taste of the alcohol," she replied.

Ralph shook his head. "You'll never make a successful alcoholic," he pronounced.

Eddie Epstein gave her tickets to the Broadway musical *Cats*. She took Greg Muldavin with her.

She reported back to her Uncle Eddie. "It was fun, Uncle Eddie. I really liked it. When will it be on television?"

Eddie repeated his pronouncement: "You'll never make a successful rich girl." He made a disapproving face.

She and Greg went to a disco in Manhattan, and she *really really* had fun, but she wound up with a pounding headache, and they couldn't get a taxi to take them back to Savage Point. The dreary wait at Penn Station killed the evening.

Other young men sought dates with her, men four and five years older than she, men who had already graduated from Ivy League colleges and held down Ivy League jobs in the city, but she didn't understand the sophisticated lingo that was meant to impress her, their studied gestures, their attempts to treat her like a duchess, their sedately hilarious tales of their wild, wild college days and boringly bloodless triumphs in business and finance. They didn't understand her, either. One actually took her to a violin recital at Lincoln Center and then expected to hop into bed with her! No way, José. The dope smelled of perfume!

But mostly she was in a mild, semiaware state of suspense, waiting for the next attack on her. Ralph Simmons stopped by four or five evenings a week to chat. He said he had adopted walking as his exercise— "It beats weightlifting"—and he needed the five-minute respite with her to recuperate. They frequently discussed what they called the "California connection."

"I still don't get it," she said. "There's nobody around here from California. And what about that sheep business?"

Ralph shook his head. "Maybe we'll never know. There have been cases of serial murders in the past where the killings suddenly stopped, and nobody ever found out who the killer was or how and why he chose his victims. Jack the Ripper was one. He picked on prostitutes."

"That's a *why*, Uncle Ralph," she said. "He had a thing about prostitutes. And in our case the killer has a thing about Honeywells and sheep, it all goes back to that. But who? That's the damn question."

As the weeks went by and nothing happened, the tensions slowly slackened. She was intelligent enough to realize that she was in a transitional phase of her life—from the abrupt end of childhood to some adult style of life that her imagination refused to envision. She drifted day to day, determined only to keep her feet on solid ground and not turn into a "phony baloney." Her view of the money she inherited was closer to that of her grandfather rather than her luxury-loving father. She refused to contemplate it, at least for the time being.

The fact of the matter was, her life during this period was dull. Not boring—she was too young and inquisitive to be bored. Just dull. And she began to feel safe. The killer had simply ceased killing.

Her visits to old Tom Shakespeare became less frequent because he repeated his stories over and over again, and she knew them all by heart. This evidence of the ravages of age and ill health saddened her at a time when she had enough sorrow to bear. Besides, if anything went seriously wrong with her Uncle Shaky, she counted on the visiting nurse to tell her.

One evening in November she was watching "Miami Vice" in her bedroom when the phone rang. She made a face and went to answer it, making a mental note to have an extension installed near her bed so she wouldn't have to leave her cozy covers and plod over the cold floor into her father's room to answer it.

"Hullo."

The voice on the phone was weak. It sounded labored. "Mona Lisa, Mona Lisa, is that you?"

A chill went through her. "Uncle Shaky?"

"It's Tom Shakespeare, Mona Lisa," the voice responded. "Can you hear me?"

"Yes! Is something the matter?"

"Probably nothing, but I . . . I . . . think something is broken. I . . . can't move."

Her mind raced like the legs of a cartoon bunny, without traction. "You're hurt?"

"That boy, that nasty one was here. You know the one. Stole the drugs."

"Brucie?" she cried in disbelief. Something in the back of her mind was saying that the whole conversation was incredible. The voice was unmistakably her Uncle Shaky's and he was in trouble, but he was saying things that didn't sound like him. "That's impossible!" she said. "He's being held in—"

"He was here, Mona Lisa," the voice said. "I can . . . use a little help. 'S probably all right, but—"

"Is he still there?" she asked.

But then she was talking into a dead line.

When she realized that Shakespeare had hung up, she exclaimed, "Oh, my God," ran back to her bedroom, took half a minute to climb into her clothes, then raced down the stairs. At the front door she paused. *A weapon,* she thought; *if Brucie's still there—* She peered around frantically. How could they have let Bruce Webster out? Was he looking for drugs again, with Uncle Shaky upstairs—? She should have taken Greg's gun when he offered it to her?! *If he's hurt Uncle Shaky, I'll shoot his balls off! See if I don't!*

She raced to the kitchen, grabbed up the largest carving knife, and ten seconds later she was in her car, starting it.

Screeching backward out of the driveway, she nearly ran over Ralph Simmons, who went sprawling on the sidewalk. "What the hell—"

She jammed on the brakes, rolled down the window, saw that Ralph was all right. "Sorry!" she said. "In a hurry! Uncle Shaky's hurt! Call you later!"

Then she shot forward in her red Firebird through the foggy darkness to go to the rescue of her grandfather's old friend Tom Shakespeare.

Tooling down Savage Point Parkway, she recalled the phone conversation. It was obvious that the old man was badly shaken. He used expressions he had never used before. He called her "Mona Lisa." He had never called her that. When he was feeling real cute, it was "Niece-a Lisa," not "Mona Lisa." And to her he had always referred to himself as "Uncle Shaky," not "Tom Shakespeare." And somehow he wouldn't say "that nasty boy." It showed how disturbed he was.

Swinging left onto Northern Boulevard, she thought *It can't be Brucie, he'd never openly defy authority by breaking out of the detox tank, he's too much of a coward for that unless—unless he's totally insane!* The carving knife was on the seat beside her. The sight of it caused a wrenching in her stomach. She imagined Brucie coming at her with a crazy look on his face—

She should have called the police. She slowed down looking for a phone booth. Then she noticed for the first time that the Savage Point security patrol car was behind her. Paulie Doran back to his old tricks! The sight of him reassured her. Paulie was a big pain in the neck, but if Bruce Webster was actually there, she and Paulie together could subdue him.

She waved when she turned off the boulevard and again when she turned onto her grandfather's street, and the patrol car followed her. Great!

Seeing no parking spaces open, she double-parked in front of her grandfather's house, clutched the carving knife, leaped out of the Firebird, and waved Paulie to a halt.

"Don't go away yet," she called. "Uncle Shaky is hurt."

Without waiting for a response, she raced up the front steps fumbling in the pocket of her jeans for her key, then paused in confusion when she saw that the front door was half open. She heard a car door chunk closed behind her and knew Paulie was following.

The hall inside the door was unlit. It was time for quick action, but it was also a time for stealth—to plunge silently into the interior darkness as ready as she could be to meet the ambush that could be awaiting her.

She waved at Paulie to follow and ran through the doorway in her sneakered feet. Emptiness. There was a light at the head of the stairs directly ahead of her, and—surprisingly—a light in her grandfather's operating room. "That damn Brucie!" she muttered, picturing him ransacking the cabinets for drugs.

Without pause, she soundlessly bounded up the stairs two at a time, and came to an abrupt halt in the doorway to her Uncle Shaky's sitting room.

Tom Shakespeare was sprawled in her grandfather's chair, his pajamas pulled askew. His round face was ashen, and blood trickled down one side of his face from a wound on his head. His eyes were fixed on a man who stood over him. The man's back was turned to Lisa, and she could note only his dark hair, short stature, broad shoulders and body, the dark green sweater he wore. Even before she could glimpse his face, she knew he was a total stranger! *The murderer was a damn stranger!*

Her peripheral vision noted another figure in the room—an inert body lying on the floor near the window.

Though it was in shadow and the face was turned away from her, she recognized it as Bruce Webster.

The tableau stunned her for a moment. The stranger was not yet aware of her presence. As she continued to gape, he moved. He raised what looked like the leg of a chair over his head, obviously about to bring it down on the old man's head.

She screamed, "Paulie!" and leaped forward. Her cry halted the downward motion of the club, and the man half turned so that she saw his face—a blunt, weather-beaten peasant's face. Her carving knife went into his shoulder, struck bone, and slewed out of her hand.

Then she was in his powerful grasp, his face close to hers, a tight smile on the lips, rage in the eyes. Apparently he, too, had dropped his weapon, for his hands, both of them, found her neck and started squeezing. The last thing she saw was the murderous rage in his eyes.

She heard Paulie shout, "No!" but the hands tightened, and blackness swept over her.

Just before she lost consciousness, she felt the hands slacken and the bulk of the stranger fall away from her.

She tried to say, "Good boy, Paulie," but couldn't. Her head hit the corner of a table as she went down.

Then nothing.

Twenty

SHE WAS BATHED in sunlight, but it was a strange kind of sunlight that had no warmth. She was a little girl out on her father's boat. Her grandfather was there, one of the few times he ventured onto his son's cabin cruiser. He was a confirmed landlubber, he said. Funny, she thought; she had never seen her grandfather swim. What was it he said? "I swim like a rock, Lisa honey. Not enough blubber. Now you," he said, pinching her plump cheek, "you'll be able to swim like Esther Williams."

She was bathed in sunlight, but she was cold. Her father was using a knife, gutting fish in the cockpit. Bluefish. Snappy little shitepokes. One of them bit her finger and drew blood. She was cold, and she was crying, and Gramps pulled her onto his lap and put his arms around her and gradually she felt warmer and safer in those protective arms, and her sobs diminished. He kissed her bitten finger up to God and said that now she had a fish story to tell her friends.

She was lying on something cold and hard. Her grandfather was gone, and instead of cuddling warmly in his lap she was flat on her back. The light filtered through her eyelids was blood-red. She squirmed and called weakly to her grandfather. She heard movements. Someone was near her. She tried to sit up and found that she couldn't. Her throat hurt. Someone had strangled her. *The stranger!* She jerked her head sideways—it spun—and she half opened her eyes.

She saw the dazzling overhead light, the white cabinets—and she knew she was lying on her grandfather's operating table! Paulie Doran was there, gazing at her with a strange look on his face.

She mumbled, "Thank you, Paulie. He was trying to kill me."

Paulie looked away.

A voice said, "Snap to it, Paolo. More faggots."

Lisa's initial impulse was to smile sleepily and say that they didn't like to be called faggots. The voice was familiar. Paulie disappeared from her sight, and there was movement under the table.

She cried, "Hey, what's going on?"

Paulie's voice: "She's awake."

The other voice: "I can hear, goldang it! Let's finish up, we don't want to take all night."

"Mr. Doran?" she said tentatively.

The blue blazer with gold buttons moved into view. The handsome face was without its customary smile. There was an aloofness there she had never seen before.

She said, "You didn't have to tie me to the table, for God's sake! I wasn't going to fall off."

"I'm afraid we had to do it, Miss Lisa," he said. The deadness in the voice chilled her.

"So untie me, damn it!"

She struggled against the bonds that tied her wrists and ankles to the clamps beneath the edges of the white metal table. She had seen her grandfather tie down animals in just this way: the clamps moved on rods and were tightened in place according to the size of the animal. The human animal Lisa was longer than any animal Gramps had ever treated; she occupied the full length of the table.

Doran said, "You can pull at them if you want to, Miss Lisa, but you'll only cut your wrists. We thought it appropriate to tie you with your grandfather's bandages. Homer Honeywell, the great lover of animals! A bandage looks flimsy as tissue paper, doesn't it? So go ahead, try to break it. You can't."

"Has everybody gone crazy?" she cried. "That man tried to kill me!" She suddenly remembered. "Uncle Shaky—he was hitting Uncle Shaky. I tried to stop him. He's the killer!"

"Examine yourself, Miss Lisa," Doran said. She noted that the exaggerated Texas accent was gone. "You broke into the house and viciously attacked Xavier from behind his back with a ten-inch knife. What does that make you?"

"Is he—is he dead?"

Doran shook his head. "No thanks to you, miss."

"But Paulie saved me."

Doran made a sour face. "Xavier has a wild temper," he said. "When he gets a sharp knife stuck in his shoulder, he tends to get mad. Without thinking, he fought back—you can't blame him—and he surely would have killed you if Paolo hadn't stopped him."

"So?"

"So he saved you for the ceremony."

"What ceremony?" she cried, feeling like Lisa in Crazyland.

"No need to get worked up," Doran said. "You'll find out."

He disappeared from her view.

Lisa lay still while her mind raced frantically. Gentleman Jack Doran, the charming lawn man from Texas, has gone out of his skull: listen, the son saves her from death, and what does the father do? He ties her to her grandfather's operating table for some sort of nutty ceremony. It has to be a joke, a cruddy, crazy joke. But Paulie wouldn't let his father actually hurt her. She and Paulie were friends, damn it!

"Paulie!" she called. "Hey, where are you, Paulie?" She kept her head turned sideways to save her eyes from the blinding light. "Paulie, what the hell's going on?"

She heard his voice. "Ask my father," it said.

"Is Uncle—is Mr. Shakespeare all right?"

"So far."

"Who is Xavier?"

The answer didn't come immediately. Then Paulie's voice said, "Our cousin from California."

Just a small turn of the kaleidoscope, and a crystalline pattern fell into place. *Oh, dear Christ,* she thought. She had laboriously studied her grandfather's letter and knew it by heart. Forgetting for the moment to be frightened, she let her excitement take over.

"By any chance," she said, "is Xavier's last name Durango?"

"Paolo," Jack Doran said sharply. "Don't talk to the girl. Get that damn wood under there. Neatly! Neatly!"

Another voice—a rough one that had to be Xavier's—came from the waiting room. "I'm bleeding like a pig," it said. "It's coming through the bandage!"

Doran's voice muttered, "Shit." Then he said louder, "Just a few more minutes, cousin. Hang in there. I got needle and suture here, we'll sew you up just fine."

"You'll give me blood poisoning, that's what you'll do!"

"Just sit there and keep your mouth clamped shut like a good fellow."

Lisa tugged gently at the bandages that bound her hands. She flexed her wrists, let her hands go limp, and in slow motion tried to wriggle her hands out of the bonds. *Think small,* she said to her hands. *Don't sweat, for God's sake,* she said to her wrists, figuring that dampness would only make the bandage material cling all that much closer to her wrists. Her hands slid partway, then the nooses became snagged at the base of her thumbs. Her damn hands were too big!

"Now the gasoline," Doran's voice said.

Lisa's heart stopped for a moment. It was all too clear what the crazy man had in mind. A family had died by fire fifty years ago. The powerful smell of gasoline filled the room. There was firewood under the table. Paulie came into view, half bent over; she couldn't see the gasoline can, but from the movements of his arms she knew he was sloshing gasoline on the wood. He kept his eyes averted from her. Then he was gone.

"Just a goddam minute!" she cried so loudly that all sounds of motion stopped.

"This crazy joke has gone far enough!" she cried. "I'm scared! Don't you see I'm frightened! Isn't that what you want? So get me off here!"

Jack Doran came into her sight. "It's no joke, Miss Lisa," he said. "It's something that has to be done. I swore to my father. He made me swear on the Bible. And that's the way it is. If it helps any, Paolo and I think you're a very nice person."

"Helps?" she exclaimed, staring at him. Then in a constricted voice she said, "You're going to burn me alive, aren't you?"

"No," he said. "Unlike your grandfather and that other devil, we're going to slay you first. It'll be quick, no pain, I promise you."

"Great! Instead of burning me alive, you're going to burn me dead! You're going to slay me first. What kind of a word is that? Slay?"

"It's a Bible word, ma'am, used in Genesis when they talk about sacrifice. That's what this is, a sort of sacrifice."

Lisa glared at him. "You're crazy, you know that?" she said.

She saw the frown form on Doran's face, the angry shake of his head, and added quickly, "If I'm the sacrifice, Mr. Doran, don't you think you ought to tell me why? Don't be in such a damn rush, that shitepoke cousin can wait, he's not gonna bleed to death. I'm the one who's gonna die—"

Even now she didn't believe her own words. The ache in her throat and the pain in her head were not intimations of fragility but rather affirmations of an indestructible young body surviving attack, surviving fire, gunshot and plane crash, too, with a vista of countless decades of pulsing life ahead.

"I'm the one who's gonna die, and I want to know *why*, damn it! You owe me!"

Doran sighed. He pulled her grandfather's barstool to him and sat down as if suddenly weary. She could see him now. "You've guessed some of it, haven't you?" he said. "You're a smart young lady, so you tell me."

Xavier's rough voice broke in, sounding closer. "What the hell you sitting down for, cousin? Light the damn fire and let's get the hell out of here! You shoulda let me finish her off! Shit, I don't understand all this farting around."

The California cousin must have been standing in the doorway of the waiting room, for Doran peered in that direction. "Go back and sit down. We'll be out of here soon enough."

Xavier's voice, retreating: "I think the lady is right. You're crazy in the head."

Doran turned his gaze back to Lisa.

She said, "Can you turn off this light, Mr. Doran? I'm getting a crick in the neck holding my head like this."

Doran said, "Paolo."

The light was switched off. The only illumination in the room came through the doorway from the outer office.

Doran said, "It wasn't until we saw the story in *People* magazine—"

Lisa said, "Never mind the damn story, start at the beginning. Start with San Ignacio. The son who was away from home at the time of the fire. Joaquin. Is that how you pronounce it? Joaquin?"

"It's not important."

"He was your father, wasn't he?"

Doran's face was in shadows, and his voice seemed to come from a long distance. "He was going to an agricultural school at a place called College Station in

Texas and living with relatives outside of town. His momma was the letter writer in the family, and when her letters stopped coming, he drove all the way back up there and saw what had happened. The house burned down. His crippled momma and his old daddy and his brother buried in the backyard. No markers. The ground was frozen, and he had to dig them up to make sure—can you picture that, Miss Lisa? And seein' the body of his old friend, the sheepdog, on the road. The sheep all gone. Well, you can imagine. . . .

"He found the man who bought the sheep, and he coaxed the facts out of him. A man named Homer Honeywell, he said—a man named Homer Honeywell sold the whole flock to him. Another rascal named San Sebastian was there, too. Both of them were gone, vamoosed. His momma had mentioned these two characters in her letters. There was no metal strongbox in the ashes of the house. It was obvious what had transpired up there in the rocky foothills of Northern California.

"I'm afraid my father used a little too much force in getting the truth out of this wool trader. The poor man accidentally expired, and my father had to hightail it out of there in a hurry. The land wasn't worth a cent in those days, so he just came away and never went back."

Jack Doran stopped talking.

Lisa said in a low voice, "I know it looked bad, Mr. Doran, and I can't blame your father for thinking what he did, but my grandfather had nothing to do with the death of those people. In fact, he tried to rescue them! I've got proof!"

"What proof is that, Miss Lisa?"

"A letter from my grandfather," she said excitedly. "It was in his safe-deposit box. What Gramps did, he ran into the house and tried to save the family, but he was too late. It's all there in the letter, I'll show it to you."

Doran smiled sadly and shook his head.

"And the dog," Lisa said louder, as if loudness made what she said more convincing. "The dog—Chico was his name—he tried to protect my grandfather and was shot by the other man, San Sebastian! Please, the letter's back home. It'll prove—"

Doran interrupted her. "It don't prove a thing," he said harshly, "except maybe Homer Honeywell had a guilty conscience. Sorry, Miss Lisa, we're wastin' time." He stood up.

"Wait!" she cried. "The least you can do is read it!"

Doran moved away from her.

She shouted, "You still haven't told me why you're doing this to *me!* I didn't kill those people! You've gone bananas, you crazy shitepoke!"

Doran sighed and came back into view. "I'm plumb talked out, Miss Lisa," he said. "Let me ask you just one question. You now have a lot of money. Where did it come from?"

"My father."

"Oh, come off it, Miss Lisa! It came from the Durango strongbox and the Durango sheep! That makes you a receiver of stolen goods, now don't it? But that's not, in actuality, the point—"

"I'll give it back," she said quickly. "Uncle Eddie says I don't know how to be a rich girl, I don't want the damn money! Listen, tomorrow morning we'll—"

Doran was shaking his head. "As I say, that's not the point. We couldn't take the money now, Miss Lisa, you can see that. Not after all that's happened. I'm afraid it wouldn't look so good. No, I think the beneficiary in all this is gonna be that nervous momma of yours. Couldn't happen to a more deserving woman," he said wryly.

Lisa's mind was wandering—from the blow on the head, her painful position on the table, the semidarkness in the room. She said, "So if it's not the money, what the hell is it? Why am I here?"

The icy coldness was back in Doran's voice. "It's very simple," he said. "You're the last of the Honeywell line. It was the oath I took. To erase Homer Honeywell and all his descendants. Make it as if he never existed. I swore in this way to avenge the honor of the Durango family."

"But—but you killed Mrs. Raymond! She wasn't a Honeywell!"

Doran sighed. "No. Technically speaking, she wasn't part of the Honeywell line. But she was your father's woman, more so than your momma in Manhattan. I confess your father made me angry, he took such great joy in spending the Durango money, especially on that show-off airplane of his. You can't imagine how enraging it was to see great chunks of our money being spent in that empty-minded way. So, I'm ashamed to say, I indulged in cruelty. I killed the woman he loved to make him grieve before we finally took care of him. I let my anger rule my head. I shouldn't have done that."

The brute face of Xavier came into her sight, saying, "Jack, for Christ's sake—"

Doran said, "You're right," and stood up.

Lisa said, "The police know all about the Durango family. They're sure to get you for murdering me and burning the house."

Doran shrugged fatalistically and spread his hands. "Maybe they will, Miss Lisa, but I don't think so. We brought a scapegoat with us. I think the police will believe the story we got cooked up for them."

"Brucie!"

"Correct. Mr. Bruce Webster. We sprung him from the calaboose, so to speak, but nobody saw us, and as far as they know he escaped and came here to finish what he started to do. You know how drug addicts are. Don't feel sorry for him, he's no good."

Lisa's mind flashed back to the scene upstairs, Bruce unconscious on the floor, Tom Shakespeare in his pajamas—

"Okay, okay," she said. "You have a reason for dragging Brucie into it, but where does Mr. Shakespeare fit into your crazy plan? If you kill him, even you have to admit it's cold-blooded murder. Let him go, Mr. Doran—"

"Can't, Miss Lisa. He's the ram caught in the thicket by his horns. He'll be part of the sacrifice, too."

"What ram? You're talking crazy!"

Upstairs, Tom Shakespeare knew he was dying. Homer's death had set the process of his own death in motion. He did not invite or welcome death, he simply awaited it. The visiting nurse had put him on a regimen of diet and exercise that might have prolonged his life indefinitely—but joylessly. The diabetes was raging within him uncontrolled, slowly diminishing one vital function after another while he indulged in one long feast of the foods he loved.

Tonight's beating was the coup de grace. He was experiencing a heart attack, a continuing one, but if there was any pain associated with it, he simply didn't feel it; perhaps the blows on the head had short-circuited the pain-sensing centers in his brain. His only sensation was an all-encompassing lassitude, a slow sinking into tepid mist.

He vaguely remembered the phone call to Lisa. His body was still capable of feeling pain, and he had made the call out of cowardice. But, thank God, he had outfoxed the savages! He had spoken in a way that would warn Lisa that he was not speaking freely. He smiled at his cleverness. But—

The glimpse of her lunging at the brutal one with a carving knife, perhaps that wasn't a delusion, after all! Dear Jesus, had his beloved Niece-a Lisa misinterpreted his signals and come racing to his rescue? Had he let himself be used as the tethered goat to lure Lisa to her death? No, it couldn't be. No . . .

He imagined he heard voices from downstairs.

He imagined he heard Lisa's voice . . .

Oh well, as his last act on earth he would go take a look if he could. No sense just lying here wasting the precious seconds. He had always liked the old saying, *He died with his boots on.* Well, this bloated old bag of self-indulgences, not booted but barefoot, would die in the act of saving the little girl who called him Uncle Shaky. Whether she was here or not didn't matter, it was something to do.

He tried to move and couldn't.

He tried again . . .

Jack Doran spoke some words she didn't understand. She heard Paulie and Xavier muttering in response. The unintelligible words fleetingly reminded her of cassocked and surpliced altar boys she had seen in a movie. But her eyes and then her whole attention were fixed on the knife that Jack Doran held before him with both hands—her carving knife!

She cried, "What are you saying? What's going on?"

Without lowering the knife, Doran said, "The Basque language is dying, I'm sorry to say. Maybe not in the mountains of the home country, but it is here. I have only a few words of it from my father, and Paolo has practically none. I feel a terrible guilt."

"That's Basque?"

Doran nodded. "That and a little Latin and maybe some Spanish. Have you made your peace with God?"

The question struck her as funny. She had had some religious training, but it had gotten lost during her rebellion. And though her father had attended the Savage Point Church as a matter of political necessity, she hadn't given a serious thought to God in years.

"You're kidding," she responded to his question.

Doran sighed sadly. "Oh, Miss Lisa—the sins of the father. Never mind, Paolo and I will say prayers for you."

Lisa struggled with her bonds, then relaxed. A peace of sorts came over her, the peace of helplessness. She wondered if her grandfather would be waiting for her. He had been a sort of god—

Her peripheral vision caught movement, and she said, "Let me see you, Paulie."

The cause of the movement retreated.

The knife was two feet above her chest.

Doran intoned something about "fire to fire," then he said, "Amen." And yet he hesitated to plunge the knife downward.

The old man swayed in the doorway. The weakness was almost absolute, but the scene before his eyes was a last call to action—Lisa tied like a dog, the knife poised over her. His misted mind worked in short erratic bursts. Homer's scalpels in cabinet. Cut loose.

Shakespeare's three-hundred-pound body moved slowly with almost glacial slowness but just as inexorably. Male voices cursed. Hands clutched at him. He was the irresistible force, gravity tugging his bulk forward and downward. His hand gripped the handle of the cabinet's glass door. He was falling. Into Doran and the table. Jack Doran was rammed downward, his wrist cracked into the metal table, and the carving knife flew out of his hand. The cabinet came from the wall. The great body knocked the table on its side, Lisa along with it. There was a scattering of flammable material. The cabinet burst open, the glass shattered, and the contents tumbled out—syringes, instruments, medicines, a can of ether. . . .

Old Tom Shakespeare had his scalpel. Sprawled on the gasoline-soaked wood, he dimly spied the bandage tying one of Lisa's wrists, and he slashed at it.

Then he died. The fatted ram caught in the thicket of firewood.

Lisa's left hand was free, but her other hand and her ankles were still tied. The table was on its side, and the knot tying her right wrist was underneath the tabletop. She couldn't reach it. The smell of gasoline was strong, suffocating.

Xavier's rough voice: "Light the damn thing, Paolo!"

And Paulie's voice said, "No." Sullenly. Defiantly.

Lisa's moment of peace was gone. Rage overtook her. Her free hand groped in the semidarkness and touched nothing but bare floor. The litter from the cabinet was behind her. "Shit, I need a miracle," she muttered to herself. Then her hand found the carving knife. She grabbed at it, cutting her hand, got a grip on the handle, and started slicing at the bandage holding her other hand—

Jack Doran was leaning over the toppled table. He had a gun in his hand. Apologetically he said, "Sorry, can't find the knife." He put the gun to her head.

Lisa slashed up with the carving knife, and buried it in his chest. Doran silently slid away from her. She tried to hang on to the knife, but Doran's body snatched it from her hand.

Significances were turned upside down. She had just killed a man and gave no thought to it. The thing that poked her passions was that the shitepoke had taken her knife! "Come back, damn it!" she shouted. *She needed that knife to free herself!*

She heard stumbling behind her, grunted curses, and knew that Paulie and the brutal cousin were tugging something out of the way. She reached up blindly with her hand and shouted, "Paulie, gimme the knife, damn it!"

The sounds stopped.

"Do you hear me, Paulie?" she called, not imploringly but imperiously, threateningly.

In the silence that followed she heard the scratch of a match.

Then *poof,* and the room was blazing.

Oh, God!

Twenty-One

RALPH SIMMONS stood in the open doorway and gaped at the scene in the waiting room. A young man and a stocky middle-aged man were dragging a third man out of the old veterinarian's operating room. He recognized the young man as the security patrolman, Jack Doran's son. Asleep on a bench was the Webster boy, the one who had attacked Lisa. *What in blazes was he doing here? He was supposed to be locked away!*

In dumb surprise, Ralph heard the older man growl something to Doran's son, then to his utter astonishment he saw the man strike a match and toss it back into the operating room. The instant conflagration spurred him to action.

He charged forward, shoved the man aside. "What the hell are you doing?" he cried. The whole operating room seemed to be on fire. The metal table was on its side as a sort of barrier to the rear, but in front of it was a jumble of blazing wood, or rather the blue fire of burning gasoline, not yet the red fire of flaming wood.

Sprawled on the fire, his pajamas just now bursting into flame, was the stout man Ralph knew as Lisa's Uncle Shaky.

"What are you doing?" Ralph cried, and started forward to drag the body from the flames. A sudden powerful shock wave threw him back, and a fireball raged over his head. The can of ether had exploded.

He was lying on the floor of the waiting room.

Off in the distance, he heard Lisa cry, "Is that you, Uncle Ralph?"

He scrambled to his feet, stunned. His eyes weren't working very well. On his second attempt he made it to the doorway. The fire was no longer confined to the jumble of wood: the whole front of the room was blazing.

"Lisa?" It was more of a squeak than a call.

He heard her voice responding, located where it was coming from. The other side of the toppled table.

The heat pushed him back. If he plunged in, he would be dead before he could get to her.

He called, "Hang on, girl!"

He turned to race out the front door, but the older man was trying to stop him.

Ralph Simmons was not a strong man and ordinarily was no match for this muscular stranger. But a sudden surge of outrage in him, combined with the weakness brought on by the loss of blood in the stranger, permitted Ralph to hurl the man backward into the blazing room. Jack Doran's son stood unmoving. Fire was licking at the door frame.

Ralph stumbled out the front door, clumped down the steps, and raced through deep shadows around the side of the house to the rear. He knew the layout dimly from the period a few years ago when his beat-up tomcat, Dizzy, had needed the old doc's attention.

He clambered over the chain-link fence, ripping his clothes, getting a painful gouge on his stomach, and falling heavily on the other side. He staggered to his feet, bounced off the fence of the animal runs, and found himself at the back door—wood with glass panels.

He rammed a foot through one of the glass panels and, being off-balance, fell flat on his back. He crawled to the door and pulled himself erect by grabbing the doorknob. In the process, he twisted the knob, and the door opened. He wagged his head groggily.

The kennel area was almost pitch-black. He found the solid wood door to the blazing room ahead of him only by the flickering red glow that seeped underneath. He groped for the knob and pulled the door open.

The heat was so intense he had to hunker down where he was shielded from the full blast of the fire by the overturned metal table. Lisa was on the floor in front of him, squirming; there were smoldering bandages on both ankles and a wrist, the fire on the other side of the table having burned them free. She was semiconscious from lack of oxygen and sounded delirious, mumbling something about a knife.

He grabbed the smoldering ankles and tugged, fell down on his backside, gained some purchase, and tugged again. He was being roasted, his strength was gone, but he had to keep tugging to stay but inches ahead of the advancing fire. Dancing devils chuckled nastily. He felt himself sliding into unconsciousness, murmured, "Oh God, no!"

The firemen found the two of them at the far end of one of the dog runs. Both were in shock and needed treatment for burns. No one had time to wonder how they had gotten there.

Twenty-Two

LISA RECUPERATED faster than Ralph Simmons. Neither of them had a clear recollection of how they had made their way to the back of the animal run, except that Lisa had strained muscles in her back, and she said, "You should lose some weight, Uncle Ralph, you really should."

None of his injuries were considered serious by the doctors. His eyebrows and much of the sparse hair on his head were gone, and his face had a ruddy, toasted look. "Shit, I look like a goddam eunuch," he grumbled when he first caught a glimpse of his face in a mirror. But it was the lingering weakness that bothered him.

"I think it's the heart," he confided to Lisa when she visited his room in the hospital.

"Bull cookies," she told him. "They say you have a heart of iron."

"Iron rusts," he said. "I'll be the first person in history to die of rust."

Lisa was permitted to roam after the first day in the hospital because her most serious burns were on her back and buttocks: the metal table, while sheltering her from the actual fire, had become a frying pan to grill her. She roamed because it wasn't much fun to lie down.

Lieutenant Carbine filled them in on the disappearance of Paulie Doran. He got the story from neighbors who had been alerted by the explosion.

"The one from next door saw you stumbling around to the back," he said to Ralph. "Then a number of them saw the Doran boy, a minute later, come out the front door carrying the Webster boy. They didn't know either of them by name. They saw the one young man carry the other young man out of the fire and lay him on the grass by the street. Then he seemed to hesitate, they said, before he loped around to the back and stood by the link fence. They say he spoke to someone."

Ralph was propped into a sitting position on the bed. Lisa stood by the window. Carbine, who was seated on a chair, looked up at her.

A memory was coming back. She had just dragged her Uncle Ralph into the dog run. Someone called, "Are you all right?" She looked and saw Paulie on the other side of the fence, and thought, *What a dumb question.*

And she had said something. What was it? She had said, "Get out of here, Paulie."

According to the witnesses, the Doran boy had then walked back to the street, gotten into the security patrol car, and driven away. The car was later found in front of the Doran house in Savage Point. His father's car was missing, presumably taken by the son.

Lieutenant Carbine said, "Do you have any idea where he might have gone, Miss Honeywell?"

An inexplicable anger came over her. "Leave Paulie alone, damn it!" she cried. "It was the father who did it all, not him!"

Carbine said calmly, "He helped his father commit three well-planned murders. He stood by while his father notified the California cousins to follow you two to this San Sebastian person and then kill him. And your Paulie is at least partly responsible for the three deaths in the fire—"

"It was me who killed Mr. Doran!" Lisa shouted. "I told you that!"

"And it was probably me," Ralph said, "who killed that murderous cousin."

Carbine stared at them. "And which one of you killed Mr. Shakespeare?"

Lisa shook her head impatiently. "You don't understand, Lieutenant. I've been thinking about it. These were Basques, and their idea of justice is different from ours. This was a vendetta, and Paulie had to obey his father. That's the way he was brought up, he couldn't help himself. You just don't understand! You're not a Basque."

Carbine had a crooked smile on his face. "No, Miss Honeywell, I'm not a Basque. My parents came from Sicily, and where do you think the word *vendetta* came from? I'm not particularly proud of the heritage, but let me just say I understand only too well."

"Then leave Paulie alone, damn it!"

The police lieutenant gazed at her for a long time. Then he said quietly, "What makes you think this Basque young man won't come back to finish the work of his father? You say he couldn't help himself. Can he help himself now? Isn't there more at stake now? In addition to the deaths of his great grandparents those many years ago, isn't there the death of his own father to be avenged? After all, you killed him, didn't you?"

"He just won't, that's all," she said stubbornly.

Bruce Webster was back at the detoxification center, reportedly shaken to the core by his near brush with death and talking of entering the ministry. *Hah,* Lisa thought.

And so Paulie and Brucie were out of her life, although there was the outside chance that one or the other might be drawn back to her with murder or rape in mind.

Lisa poopoohed the danger. "I can handle them," she said in her old happy-go-lucky way.

But her friends worried.

It was Eddie Epstein who came up with the solution that put their minds at rest.

On Christmas Eve when Lisa and Greg were outside in the chill evening looking back and admiring the garish display of lights with which they had covered the front of the house—Ralph had muttered to Lillian that it looked like "a pizza palace"—Eddie Epstein arrived with his present for her, a large box with Christmas wrappings on it.

They went inside, and Lisa opened it, sitting on the floor by the fireplace.

Epstein said, "It's just what you need—a fierce watchdog."

Lisa hugged the fluffy little puppy, laughing like a child.

Ralph Simmons looked on with a rueful smile, thinking that he had been Lisa's watchdog for a while and had nearly gotten her killed. He hoped the dog would be more diligent in guarding his precious charge, the last of the Honeywells.